Acting Edition

Toni Stone

An Original Play

by Lydia R. Diamond

Based on *Curveball, The Remarkable Story of Toni Stone* by Martha Ackmann

⫴SAMUEL FRENCH⫴

FOR PRODUCTION INQUIRIES

UNITED STATES AND CANADA
info@concordtheatricals.com
1-866-979-0447

UNITED KINGDOM AND EUROPE
licensing@concordtheatricals.co.uk
020-7054-7298

Each title is subject to availability from Concord Theatricals Corp., depending upon country of performance. Please be aware that *TONI STONE* may not be licensed by Concord Theatricals Corp. in your territory. Professional and amateur producers should contact the nearest Concord Theatricals Corp. office or licensing partner to verify availability.

This work is published by Samuel French, an imprint of Concord Theatricals Corp.

MUSIC AND THIRD-PARTY MATERIALS USE NOTE

IMPORTANT BILLING AND CREDIT REQUIREMENTS

TONI STONE was commissioned by Roundabout Theatre Company and Samantha Barrie and originally produced by Roundabout Theatre Company, New York, New York in association with Samantha Barrie, premiering on May 23, 2019. The director was Pam MacKinnon, with lighting design by Allen Lee Hughes, costume design by Dede Ayite, set design by Riccardo Hernández, hair and wig design by Cookie Jordan, original music and sound design by Broken Chord, choreography by Camille A. Brown, and fight direction by Tom Schall. The production stage manager was Charles M. Turner III. The cast was as follows:

TONI STONE	April Matthis
ALBERGA	Harvy Blanks
MILLIE	Kenn E. Head
STRETCH	Eric Berryman
KING TUT	Phillip James Brannon
SPEC	Daniel J. Bryant
ELZIE	Jonathan Burke
WOODY	Ezra Knight
JIMMY	Toney Goins
U/S ALBERGA, MILLIE	Melvin Abston
U/S TONI STONE	Jennean Farmer
U/S ELZIE, JIMMY, SPEC	Alex Joseph Grayson
U/S WOODY, STRETCH, KING TUT	Damian Thompson

TONI STONE made its West Coast premiere at the American Conservatory Theater in San Francisco, California on March 11, 2020. The performance was directed by Pam MacKinnon, with scenic design by Riccardo Hernández, costume design by Dede Ayite, lighting design by Allen Lee Hughes, sound design and original music by Broken Chord, hair and wig design by Cookie Jordan, choreography by Camille A. Brown, and associate choreography by Jay Staten. The production stage manager was Elisa Guthertz, the dramaturg was Allie Moss, and the casting director was Janet Foster. The cast was as follows:

TONI STONE	Dawn Ursula
ALBERGA / RUFUS	Ray Shell
MILLIE / WILLIE	Kenn E. Head
STRETCH / SYDNEY	Sean-Maurice Lynch
KING TUT / SUPERVISOR	JaBen Early
SPEC / GABBY	Daniel J. Bryant
ELZIE	Rodney Earl Jackson Jr.
WOODY / MOTHER	Jarrod Smith
JIMMY / FATHER O'KEEFE	Marquis D. Gibson

TONI STONE received development support from the Resident Artists Program at Arena Stage, Washington, D.C., with the production at Arena Stage, meant to run from September 3 – October 3, 2021, cut short due to a health issue. The director was Pam MacKinnon, with lighting design by Allen Lee Hughes, costume design by Dede Ayite, set design by Riccardo Hernández, hair and wig design by Cookie Jordan, original music and sound design by Broken Chord, and choreography by Camille A. Brown. The stage manager was Elisa Guthertz and the casting director was Victor Vazquez. The cast was as follows:

TONI STONE	Santoya Fields
ALBERGA / RUFUS	Aldo Billingslea
MILLIE / WILLIE	Kenn E. Head
STRETCH / SYD	Sean-Maurice Lynch
KING TUT	Jaben Early
SPEC / GABBY	Gilbert Lewis Bailey II
ELZIE	Rodney Earl Jackson Jr.
WOODY / MOTHER	Jarrod Mims Smith
JIMMY / FATHER O'KEEFE	Deimoni Brewington

CHARACTERS

TONI STONE – (28-35, Black) Highly personable, athletic, and quirky. When Toni is in Jack's, or with Millie, she wears a man's blazer over her uniform, and a Stetson hat.

PLAYERS – Eight to ten Black male actors make up the ensemble (Players). They play various characters to be determined by the director.

Once a "Player" is assigned a role, he plays that role consistently.

ALBERGA – (a young and sexy 64, Black) Toni's eventual husband.

MILLIE – (anywhere between mid-thirties to late forties, Black) Toni's "female" confidant.

Casting Notes:

I would suggest that the actor cast as Woody not be the darkest brown member of the cast, as this can sometimes tilt into stereotype. Additionally, I'd urge you to consider casting/playing Elzie as not "effeminate" – to avoid both the pitfalls of stereotyping, and more importantly, to deepen and enrich the storytelling.

At the production's discretion, two extra actors, dedicated to playing only Alberga and Millie, may be cast. (But not if it requires casting fewer than eight male actors as "Players.")

SETTING

Various locations
1920-1940s USA

AUTHOR'S NOTE

There are far too many brilliant, creative, and generous people who, over the years, have lent their talents and support to the creation of this play. I've had the privilege of working with insightful dramaturgs, actors who have remained committed to this project over the course of many years of workshops, institutions that have provided the space and resources for development, and friends and family whose encouragement has often saved me from myself. I offer here a list, in no particular order, of only a fraction of the names of those who have touched this project and to whom I will be forever grateful: Henry Perkins, Jocelyn Clarke, Dana Formby, Waylon Wood, Uzo Aduba, April Matthis, Marsha Estell, Michelle Wilson, Penelope Walker, Charlette Speigner, Nambi E. Kelley, Joy Meads, Jill Rafson, The Radcliffe Institute at Harvard, The Arena Stage, Marie Scott, The McCarter Theatre Company's Sally B. Goodman Artist Retreat, Chuck Smith, Chicago Dramatists, Eric Simonson and the Door Kinetic Arts Festival, JT Rogers, John Weidman, Kenn E. Head, Ezra Knight, Daniel Bryant, Megan Sandberg-Zakian, Ron O.J. Parson, Beverly Morgan-Welch, Robert Barry Fleming, Chuck Cohen, Roundabout Theatre Company, and American Conservatory Theatre.

And a special thanks to: Marie Scott – for quite literally carrying me over the finish line; my Agent, Derek Zasky; Nicole Matte and Concord Theatricals (for patience and forgiveness as I sat on the galleys – always a doe in the headlights of the permanence of publication).

Martha Ackmann, thank you for giving us *Curveball*, the definitive biography of Toni Stone and where the seeds of this project were sewn. Thank you Samantha Barrie for bringing this project to me, and producing it with such dedication and tenacity. Thank you Pam MacKinnon, my partner in crime.

Thank you Baylor, for being my son. And thank you Beverly Holmes, for being my mom.

ACT I

*(**TONI STONE** stands in a tight spot down center.)*

TONI. *(To audience.)* It is round, and small, and it fits right there in your hand. And it's not the thing itself, it's the weight of it. It's how it feel, and how it fills what your hand was without it. Before that weight, my hand, your hand, is just a thing that serves you. It is a tool, no better than a fork or a screwdriver. Before the weight, it...my hand, your hand, our hands are only there to pick up or tie or brush off or put down or move a thing. And then there is this...

> *(A single baseball rolls in slowly, stopping magically right in front of **TONI**.)*
>
> *(Beat.)*
>
> *(She picks it up.)*

...And it feels right. It feels like what your hand, my hand, wanted all along.

> *(Upstage, in low light, a **BASEBALL PLAYER** in a dusty, well-worn uniform pantomimes hitting a ball in slow motion. He watches the ball go up and up, and takes his stance to hit again. Through the following, each of the other seven **PLAYERS** enter one at a time, spreading out across the stage and joining the first **PLAYER**, batting in unison. **TONI** does not wait for each to establish.)*

I knew this girl once...people had told me she was a pretty girl. My mother had told me she was pretty. And she, my mama, tried to push us to play together...

because, I guess she thought some of that pretty would rub off on me. *(Add next* **PLAYER.***)* But I'm trying to tell you about the weight. Of a thing... So this girl. This girl they says is pretty...and I think she was. Yes. She was pretty. But that ain't the story. It's the ball. I am trying to tell you about the weight of it, in a hand...yes. *(Add next two* **PLAYERS.***)* So this girl. She, I guess, don't see me too good. Or maybe it all she know how to talk 'bout. And she's nice, and she's trying to be friendly, 'cause her mama talked to my mama and she's supposed to be a good influence or some such. And what I'm trying to say is, she talk about boys like without them a piece of her is missing. *(Add next* **PLAYER.***)* And I try to hear her, I do, because she a nice girl. An' she always want to tell me about this one or that one or this one an' I don't understand. But then yesterday, really, just yesterday, *(Add next* **PLAYER.***)* I'm doin' circles, jess making my arm warm and loose and I throw the ball, and it's gone.

> *(Beat.)*

And I miss it. An' it seem like the same. Like what this is is what the boys are for this girl, this pretty girl, I'm sorry I don't recall her name... Seem like what my life is, is about having it in my hand, when it come in hard and sting, or when it drop in an' jess lay there. Sweetly. *(Add final two* **PLAYERS.***)* When it come and go so fast it feel like it never was there. This is what I need. What I good at. What I do better than anybody. What I know better than anybody. Better maybe than this girl know boys.

> *(The* **PLAYERS** *stop, watch the balls fly; their light fades as they lower the bats to their sides.)*

The weight of it, in my hand.

> *(Lights rise, revealing a stage of various levels, of various hues of aged wood, and set pieces comprised of various elements from a baseball field: lockers, benches, bleachers,*

piles of equipment, chain-link fencing, etc. From this the **PLAYERS** *build scenes, using baseball equipment as props, e.g. a catcher's mask becomes a bowl on a table, a glove becomes a woman's hat, etc. All prop and costume pieces are housed on the stage.)*

(Note: Some consistent visual and/or physical gesture turns Black players into Whites, e.g. a player's hat is turned inside out to reveal a bright-white lining, or a player's jersey is turned inside out.)

I'm not a big talker. I talk a lot, but I don't talk big. I have pride, but I wouldn't say I'm proud. I don't put more in a story then is really there. And I don't like it when other people do. So don't think I'm bragging when I tell you that I do the things I do well, better'n anybody. I am prone to ramblin'. Never could tell a story from beginning to end all nice and neat. My brain don't work that way.

(Beat.)

Now what was it I was fixin' to tell you...see what I mean.

(Beat.)

I wanna tell you somethin' 'bout...

(Sound of a bat hitting a ball... Cast members, including **TONI**, *watch the ball go up and up... In a synchronized slow-motion, the* **PLAYERS** *spot it, follow it, and reach, freezing in the reach.)*

(The sound of the ball hitting **TONI**'*s glove... She removes the ball from the glove.)*

Reaching.

(The **PLAYERS** *have receded to the edges of the stage, always invested in the action of the scene. They are telling this story together.)*

TONI. I'm telling you about reaching. And me. That's why I
think you're here. So I can tell you about me. Because,
you may have heard, I am the first woman to ever play
professional ball. Don't know why it was me and not
someone else. Don't know even if history will think it
matters. But you do maybe, or you wouldn't be there
and I wouldn't be here so...

 (Beat.)

Ohhh but first...my boys...you should meet my boys. I
call 'em that, but I don't think you allowed to call them
that. Yes, *you* can't call 'em that. They men, through
and through, each and every one. Have to fight every
second of every day to be men... But they're my boys.
The Indianapolis Clowns. But first...meet Sydney
Pollock. He's White.

 *(The **PLAYER** who will play **SYD** steps forward*
 and "turns" White. This establishes what the
 vocabulary for turning White will be.)

He's the owner of the Clowns. Nice man, good heart,
pays better than the other owners, White or Black. He
takes as good a care of us as any White man would
think he should. Still, you hear what I said? He the
owner. He own us.

SYD. Someone once asked me, why own a Negro team
when I can well afford a piece of the majors. It's
simple. Baseball is as serious a sport as there is. But
let's be honest. It's also entertainment. Negro Leagues
understand this. I like show business, I like baseball,
and, I like Negroes.

 *(He morphs back into one of the **PLAYERS**.)*

SPEC. *(To **TONI**.)* Also, Whites can always smell where
there's money to be made, and Negroes always happy
to spend money on whatever Whites are selling –

TONI. So, these my boys from the Indianapolis Clowns...

(Each **PLAYER** *comes forward at the sound of his name until they are all lined up downstage, just behind* **TONI**.*)*

Rufus McNeal – utility man – and 'cause he can play, an' 'cause he ain't never said nothin' bad 'bout nobody, he don't get razzed...mostly he don't get in it at all. Jimmy Wilkes, he our greenest, play flashy, play hard, now if we can just get him to stop playing stupid.

JIMMY. Hey!!

TONI. Willie Brown – left field – on the field he's solid – otherwise he pretty much in his own world where a bottle keep him company. Willie Gaines, our catcher, team manager, and coach. We call him Stretch, so he won't be confused with drunk Willie, and 'cause it don't matter where the ball go, it's gonna end up in his glove and he ain't gone move an inch.

STRETCH. It's true.

TONI. He's a young person with an old way about him. He's also one of my favorite people.

STRETCH. Thank you Miss Stone.

TONI. My pleasure Mr. Stretch.

WOODY. This what we doin' today?

TONI. Woody Bush –

(Beat.)

I'll just let him show hisself – you'll see. Elzie Marshall – popular with the ladies, *(***JIMMY** *giggles.)* though the boys joke he's compensating. Far as I'm concerned all [that] matter is that he's the toughest left-hander I ever met. King Tut...he our clown, a comic genius, most famous person on the team, most famous person in the Negro Leagues, some would say he an institution –

KING. You makin' me sound old Toni. *(Clowning.)* I is, I is old – but in baseball years. Tha's young in regular people years. But I is also the most handsomest, mosted talentedest, all round the mostededest –

TONI. – But don't let his clownin' fool you...he can play...we all come to play. And last but not least 'course, there's Spec Beebop short on legs, long on brains. In another life, he'd have been a University Professor. But you get the life you get. And I like about Spec, that he seems happy with all that God did and didn't give him. Spec.

> (**SPEC** *is totally absorbed in a book.*)

Spec! SPEC!

> (*Through the following,* **SPEC** *clumsily gathers his book and rushes to his place in the line.*)

Unlike Elzie, Spec's exploits with the opposite sex are well documented and border on legendary.

SPEC. *(To audience.)* A man's worth is not measured by the length of his penis.

> (*Beat.*)

Unless you measure it.

TONI. You don't need to try to remember their names. It matters that I tell you though...'cause if I don't, history ain't much tryin' to remember 'em.

> (*Beat.*)

So, I'ma need you to keep up. Because where I'm taking you lives between the reach and the weight of a ball.

> (*Beat beat.*)

Wait, I shouldn't just be assuming y'all know anything 'bout the game. There's basic things you gotta know.

> (*Light and sound become bright, upbeat. Through this the* **PLAYERS** *build the field and dugout. This is a highly choreographed acting out of the kind of physical prowess and smart teamwork required to play at the highest level. Chairs are tossed from one to another, a dugout formed, etc. We see the incredible showmanship that must accompany the regular requirements of the game.*)

SPEC. Keep in mind that baseball is a science.

KING. Yeah, we play silly, we play hard, we play pretty, AND we play smart.

WOODY. That's what separates the good players from the bad.

STRETCH. And only thing separates the good players from the great, is that they don't have the privilege of wearing these jerseys we got on what say "Clowns."

SPEC. You all know about three bases, three outs, nine players, and nine innings, tops and bottoms.

JIMMY. Ask Elzie to tell you 'bout tops and bottoms.

*(Silence. **JIMMY**'s attempt at ribbing **ELZIE** has gone too far and fallen flat.)*

KING. LORD help this simple boy for he know not what he sayith.

STRETCH. Ever.

(Beat.)

You were saying Spec.

*(Each **PLAYER** "takes the field" when his position is named. At some point the actors shift, "rotating the field.")*

SPEC. You got your pitcher, catcher, first base, second base –

TONI.   **WOODY**.

That's mine.   That's mine.

TONI. ...Covers between second and first, in best position for short hard drives up the middle, gotta have a fast arm, a good eye, gotta know where to get the ball and get it there fast.

WOODY. Requires a strong arm.

TONI. Fine, 'cause I got two strong arms.

WOODY. Two strong arms, my ass.

JIMMY. *(Giggling.)* Asssss... Elzie –

STRETCH. Jimmy, shut up. Can't mess with people who are bigger'n play better'n you.

(JIMMY's *deflated again.*)

TONI. See, that's Stretch. He's got a certain kind of...what was that word, Spec?

SPEC. Gravitas.

TONI. Gravitas. Nice, right? Means whatever's comin' out of his mouth comes out like you need to hear it, and you wanna listen.

WOODY. Jesus Christ... Spec's short, read books, King's funny, Jimmy stupid, Stretch tall, Willie drunk, Elzie pretty, and Toni a girl. Goddammit, can we do this? King –

KING. Third, shortstop, left field, center, and right.

SPEC. Three outs, three bases, nine innings –

ALL. Nine players,

KING. Ball's about nine inches round...

SPEC. For a normal-sized person that's the size of the palm of your hand. For someone like me... Short in stature maybe, but endowed with large hands, large feet, and a large...

TONI. Spec!

STRETCH. The bases form a ninety-foot diamond.

WOODY. End of field fence is about three hundred feet from home plate.

STRETCH. Each side of home plate, twelve inches long –

KING. The bases are ninety feet apart –

ELZIE. Pitcher's mound's a circle, fifteen inches high, nine feet across, the middle of it is sixty feet, six inches from home plate, atop the middle is the rubber –

JIMMY. (*Giggling.*) Rubber...

ELZIE. Rubber's twelve inches on each side –

SPEC. Anyway, it's all divisible by three.

KING. That's a trinity man. That's religion.

STRETCH. Yep. We takin' you to church tonight.

(*Beat.*)

So that's what it is.

ALL. This what we do.

TONI. We win and we bring the show.

> *(A short, vaudevillian-like choreographed number ensues. It ends with all of the **PLAYERS** on one knee, a baseball glove on each hand, giving the Al Jolson jazz hands. **TONI** steps out from behind them.)*

That's the reach we have to do to get to the thing we're here to do. Now, you need to know Jack's.

> *(The **PLAYERS** transform a corner of the stage into Jack's Tavern. **TONI** dons a man's suit jacket and Stetson hat that she always wears when off the field. The **PLAYER** who will be **ALBERGA** dons a Stetson and suit jacket as well.)*

ALBERGA. And Alberga.

TONI. And Alberga. You need to know Alberga. *(To audience.)* I met Alberga at Jack's.

> *(Beat.)*

Jack's Tavern's a small, smoky, steamy place. From the minute I got to town, Jack's was my home away from home.

> *(Some **PLAYERS** sit, others become male/female **COUPLES** and slow dance on the floor.)*

Windows all fogged up from the hot breath of the boys trying to talk up the ladies who act like they got all dressed up an' sat down at the bar 'cause they was thirsty...the dance floor is nothin' more'n a dark corner on the way to the bathroom, room enough though for jitterbugs and hops that calm down into slow grinds while the jukebox jukes. Jack's is a lot like little southern churches with ministers in shiny Stacy Adams who drive Cadillacs and have pretty wives in big hats in the front row, and young girls on the side what sit in the choir. Except for the hats, it's all pretty much the same. Ceremony...the things you know 'cause you understand the language of a place. The rules. I have to have rules I can sink my teeth into.

> *(She makes her way to the bar, where* **ALBERGA** *nurses a drink. She doesn't notice him.)*

(To audience.) If Jack's the church *(Takes a sip.)* this is communion.

> *(Beat.)*

I like to be at the bar, where I can go over whatever game I picked up that day. *(Gesturing to disinterested* **BARTENDER**.*)* She don't care what I'm saying, but she there, and can't go nowhere.

(To **BARTENDER**.*)* So, at the top of the third, we had them squeezed, all they could do is put in their lefty... But our pitcher was too good to let someone standing on the wrong side of home get him off his game...after that...

ALBERGA. You're that baseball girl.

TONI. *(Still to* **BARTENDER**.*)* – After that things pretty much fell into place. We had a hot-shot, blue-black shortstop, plays for the Negroes, but barnstorms off season. One of the best switch-hitters I've ever seen. There's also this baby-face mulatto who works in the mines and can hit a pebble in a typhoon.

ALBERGA. Must be good with a real ball then.

> *(***TONI*** gives him a look...not quite getting the joke.)*

TONI. *(To* **BARTENDER**.*)* Anyway, we kicked their asses.

> *(Beat.)*

ALBERGA. You're the baseball girl I hear about.

TONI. Yes. And you're that half-Jamaican businessman that owns everything.

ALBERGA. I'm the half-Jamaican businessman that owns what I own, not everything. Auralious Alberga.

TONI. Toni Stone. *(Shaking hands.)* It's nice to meet you Mr. Alberga.

ALBERGA. Auralious.

    (Beat.)

Very nice suit.

TONI. Thanks. Got it at Perry's, corner of Filmore and Grove.

ALBERGA. I've frequented that shop.

TONI. I like that they tailor for free.

ALBERGA. Heard you throw better than a man, and can turn a double play for breakfast.

TONI. Yep. You always in here giving out those signs and pamphlets. You own everything AND you're a politician?

ALBERGA. I'm...involved in civic matters.

TONI. Civic. You mean you think you can tell them White folks to care about us? 'Cause they don't.

ALBERGA. Agreed. But it's our city too. We pay taxes.

TONI. I don't. Why would I do that?

ALBERGA. So you don't go to jail. You can't vote from jail.

TONI. I don't vote, and I don't like people telling me what to do.

ALBERGA. I'm sorry, if I...was presumptuous. If I help you with your taxes will you go down with me and vote?

TONI. You'll do my taxes *and* look after my books?

ALBERGA. You don't know me from Adam, but you want me in your money?

TONI. I don't know anyone named Adam. But you seem honest and you have a lot of money, and I don't have any to speak of, so no reason to steal mine.

ALBERGA. Then why do you need a moneyman?

TONI. Oh, I plan to have money. Soon.

ALBERGA. If I take care of the money you're anticipating, you'll vote?

TONI. Who I'm supposed to vote for?

ALBERGA. The right people.

TONI. How I know who that is?

ALBERGA. I'll tell you.

TONI. So you tell all these folks up in here what to do and they do it?

ALBERGA. Yes. Because I've proven myself.

TONI. I can see what you're saying.

ALBERGA. Your glass is empty.

TONI. *(A little defensively.)* So?

ALBERGA. May I buy you another?

TONI. Oh. No. Thank you.

ALBERGA. You hungry?

TONI. No.

> *(A long beat while **ALBERGA** takes in the completely unaffected **TONI**.)*

ALBERGA. So I hear you don't just play with the big boys, but you're better than half of them. You're on a team?

TONI. No. Not yet. I pick up games here and there when I can. I ain't been in town but a minute, but I have proven myself too. Whenever a team need a man to stand in, I get a call.

> *(**PLAYERS** transform the bar into Mother's porch.)*

(To audience.) So yeah. I play with "the big boys." Only ever did play with boys, even when I was a little girl.

> *(She settles onto the ground and takes baseball cards out of her pocket, using them like flash cards as she arranges them on the ground in front of her. She watches **MOTHER** cross.)*

(To audience.) I'm a little girl. These are my baseball cards. Buy 'em on the sly with church money. Babe Ruth – Yankees. Pitcher/outfield. 145 games. Forty-nine home runs. Lou Gehrig, also New York Yankees. First base. Forty-one home runs. Mel Ott – New York Giants. Right field/third base. 148 games. Twenty-five home runs.

*(To audience and **ALBERGA**.)* That's Mother.

MOTHER. Father O'Keefe.

TONI. That's church.

> (*A* **PLAYER** *turns White, into* **FATHER O'KEEFE.**
> *Through the following,* **TONI** *observes.*)

FATHER O'KEEFE. (*Irish accent.*) Thank you for making time to see me Mrs. Stone...

MOTHER. I'm sorry my husband couldn't be here... Saturdays are busy down at the shop...

FATHER O'KEEFE. No. No need to explain Mrs. Stone.

MOTHER. May I offer you a beverage Father?

FATHER O'KEEFE. (*Amused.*) Ahh, word gets around.

MOTHER. (*Embarrassed.*) That's not at all what I... Just, I have some coffee...or tea, it could be tea...

FATHER O'KEEFE. No, I really only have a few minutes... Could we sit for a moment?

> (*They sit.*)

It's about your girl, Tomboy.

MOTHER. Marcenia.

TONI. (*To audience.*) Yes, Marcenia. Let's please keep that to ourselves.

FATHER O'KEEFE. Apologies... Yes, Marcenia...

TONI. (*To audience.*) I was always getting in trouble in Sunday school.

MOTHER. What has she gotten herself into now?

TONI. (*Playing with cards.*) Hank Greenberg – Detroit Tigers. First base. Fifty-eight home runs. Arky Vaughan – Pittsburgh Pirates. Shortstop. Forty-nine home runs.

MOTHER. Perhaps we should have that beverage Father O'Keefe...

> (*She exits.*)

TONI. The problem was I had to sit still too damn long, and half the time what they talking about don't make logical sense. Now I do believe in God, and I'm even okay with the idea that Jesus is the Son of God. It's a reach, but sometimes you gotta reach. But I would always get stuck on the idea that all the people that don't believe in it all, the way we do, will go to hell. First, seemed like God, being benevolent and everything, wouldn't let all those people that just didn't get born where there are Christians, or maybe they're Jewish or Sanctified or something, it just wouldn't make sense for them to have to be in hell with the people that hate and kill people who look like me. Or who hate and kill anybody for any reason. And then there's earthquakes, and floods, and wars and famines...and I would get stuck on all that and ask, just trying to work it out...but Sunday school teachers don't like wiggly girls who ask too many questions.

(**MOTHER** *returns with two glasses of iced tea.*)

MOTHER. Sweet tea. And I put in a little something to sweeten it further, if you are not opposed.

FATHER O'KEEFE. I appreciate your hospitality Mrs. Stone.

(*They settle on a bench.*)

(*Beat.*)

MOTHER. So, what has she done this time Father?

FATHER O'KEEFE. You've misunderstood. Marcenia hasn't done anything wrong.

MOTHER. She hasn't?

(**TONI** *stops, leans in.*)

FATHER O'KEEFE. She has distinguished herself in the best way. Several weeks ago Marcenia agreed to step into a game, you know we have a parish baseball team, such as it is... I should have asked you first –

MOTHER. Probably, yes...

FATHER O'KEEFE. ...But we were down a boy and she's always there, and I thought...let's see what she has.

MOTHER. Distinguished herself how?

FATHER O'KEEFE. The boys finally got a taste of winning and decided it was infinitely better than what they thought would be the humiliation of being outplayed by a girl. So they want her to stay.

MOTHER. Marcenia's father and I have been encouraging her to pursue more suitable activities.

TONI. *(To audience.)* Daddy didn't care one way or the other.

FATHER O'KEEFE. More suitable activities for a girl?

MOTHER. For a Negro child who must make a living in this world...

FATHER O'KEEFE. Shouldn't all parents simply want children who are happy and engaged in those things at which they excel naturally?

MOTHER. Father I do realize that you spend a lot of your time caring for the huddled masses. Marcenia's father and I are not huddled. Baseball will not put food on Marcenia's table.

> *(Beat.)*

FATHER O'KEEFE. If I may... I see that Marcenia, struggles to find her place.

TONI. *(To audience.)* Mother Mary of Joseph here it comes.

MOTHER. Girls without a source of income become women who find money in unfortunate ways.

TONI. *(To audience.)* Girls without a source of income become women who find money in unfortunate ways. Always seemed to me that if you find some money, just come up on some money...that would be very fortunate.

FATHER O'KEEFE. Mrs. Stone, I would simply ask that you consider letting the Church be a place where her God-given talents might be nurtured. We can both agree that Marcenia is very special.

TONI. *(To audience.)* Father O'Keefe is the only person I think ever really meant "special" when he called me "special."

> *(Through this, **TONI** and the lights shift to mid-conversation at the bar with **ALBERGA** in Jack's Tavern.)*

ALBERGA. You are special.

TONI. *(To audience.)* Well. They put me in a *special* school, with *special* students, who couldn't hardly count from one to ten, and teachers who talked to us like we was five. Soon as people tell you there's something wrong with your mind, you believe it.

(Joining **ALBERGA.***)* That's why I like you Alberga. You got this way of making anyone you talk to feel almost as smart as you are.

ALBERGA. That's because I only talk to smart people.

TONI. Then I don't know why you here with me.

ALBERGA. I find your encyclopedic knowledge of anything that's ever happened on a baseball field, anywhere in the western world, dazzling.

TONI. Well, not *anywhere...*in the western world. There are a lot of places I don't know about, and teams I haven't heard of... It would not be accurate to say I know about everything that's happened in baseball everywhere.

(To audience.) It's true, I could keep every stat of every player, who I know about, who's ever played ball on any team, that I know about, and tell you what angle a ball would fly off a bat and how fast depending on how the batter stands, and which way the wind was blowing. Daddy tried to make me see how that was algebra, or geometry...

ALBERGA. That's physics.

TONI. Whatever it was, I could not substitute the bucket of apples that Mrs. Smith must sell for fifty cents a bushel and why or how I should care what it might mean if that bucket was divided into four and two oranges or some such is added to it... Made no sense. And I would say to my daddy, "If I want an apple, or a bushel of apples, I will ask the merchant how much it costs, and I will pay for exactly that much if it sounds reasonable... or I will decide to forgo the apple that day."

(To **ALBERGA.***)* So that's not smart. That's just a thing I can do.

(**ALBERGA** *gestures to her glass, offering* **TONI**
another drink.)

ALBERGA. Will you have another?

TONI. Why do you care so much what's in my glass?

ALBERGA. A man wants to buy a woman a drink because it's
something we can give.

(**MILLIE***'s light comes on.*)

MILLIE. That's only part of why a man buys a woman a drink.

TONI. *(To* **MILLIE.***)* Well wait. It's not your turn yet.

(*To audience.*) You'll know Millie soon enough.

(**MILLIE***'s light goes off.*)

ALBERGA. It's a gesture. It says to a woman, you please me,
I like you, I would like to spend time with you...

(**MILLIE***'s light comes back on.*)

MILLIE. It also says I would like to get you shit-faced to the
moon so I can get those drawers down.

TONI. Millie, please. Not now.

(**MILLIE***'s light goes out.*)

(*To* **ALBERGA.***)* Wouldn't you save a lot of money and
time if instead of forcing a woman to drink, you just
would say to her, "You please me, I like you, I would
like to spend time with you." 'Cause maybe she just isn't
thirsty, and then you would be thinking she doesn't
appreciate the nice things you wanting for her to
know...

ALBERGA. You are literal.

TONI. Yes I am. And you've seen that I only drink one drink.
And then I leave. And I'm finished now. So it was very
nice speaking with you again.

(*And with that, she's gone.*)

(*To audience.*) I told you how I don't tell a story all nice
and neat. The team, the rules, Alberga...Millie, kind of,
more on that later, Mother, Father O'Keefe, Jack's...

UMPIRE. *(Offstage.)* STRIKE THREE!

TONI. The game! Let's play ball with my Clowns.

> *(Light shifts. **TONI** joins the team in the dugout built by the **PLAYERS** during the preceding scene.)*
>
> *(The Clowns are up to bat in a losing game.)*
>
> *(**JIMMY** enters the dugout. **WOODY** trips him.)*

WOODY. Why you playing like Jackie Robinson Jimmy?

TONI. Callin' someone Jackie's s'posed to be an insult Woody?

WOODY. Stay out of it Toni.

TONI. How you gone get on Jimmy for a game we all 'bout to lose? You up King.

> *(**KING** grabs his bat and leaves the dugout.)*

And, how you gonna do it talkin' trash 'bout someone you wish you was?

STRETCH. All y'all shut up and get your heads in the game. That's why we losin' now.

WOODY. *(To **STRETCH**.)* Oh, is that why? I thought it was 'cause the ball's allergic to your bat today.

TONI. Woody, respect. He our coach.

WOODY. He ain't coach. He ain't nothin' but the Negro what hand out the paychecks from that White man and drive the bus. We losin' 'cause y'all mothafuckas woke up today like you got the amnesia and ain't never seen a baseball.

> *(They all stop and watch **KING**. Crack of the bat. He has connected. They watch it go up, hopeful, but...)*

UMPIRE. *(Offstage.)* STRIKE ONE!

STRETCH. DAMN!

TONI. That's alright. We still in it.

JIMMY. Woody, why you all the time hatin' on Jackie?

WOODY. It's fucked up White people think Jackie's best we got.

(**KING** *swings again. They watch it go up.*)

UMPIRE. *(Offstage.)* STRIKE TWO!

SPEC. Hey y'all, listen to this.

TONI. *(To audience.)* Yes. Spec brings all his books into the dugout.

SPEC. "It is a peculiar sensation..."

TONI. A sensation? Where? You want we get you a doctor for that?

SPEC. No, listen... W.E.B. Du Bois, "peculiar sensation... measuring one's soul by the tape of a world that looks on in amused contempt and pity."

JIMMY. Always talking about measuring things...

UMPIRE. *(Offstage.)* STRIKE THREE!

STRETCH. Mark my words...a hundred years from now they'll be talkin' 'bout they hired Jackie for his fortitude and disposition.

(**KING** *returns to the dugout.*)

KING. Y'all still talking about Jackie?

ELZIE. It help him he ain't bad to look at. *(Covering.)* That's what some of my women be tellin' me. Somethin' 'bout his chin.

WOODY. What Negro what's alive today ain't got fortitude?

(**STRETCH** *grabs his bat, shuffles off.*)

King, how many times this week you get called a nigger?

KING. *(For the team, in his exaggerated Step-N-Fetchit voice.)* I don't be knowin' nothin' 'bout no countin'... I jess hit at the round thing wiff dis here stick. Ain't even knowed whachu tryin' to say. I ain't got Jackie's disposition. I's happy here in the Negroes wiff my own people. Might get overcome if I gots to play wiff dem real talented White folks what can hit those lil white balls so far an' run so fast.

(**STRETCH** *has swung and missed.*)

UMPIRE. *(Offstage.)* STRIKE ONE!

(Beat.)

TONI. Elzie, didn't Jackie get three hits off of you in Kansas last year?

ELZIE. I done told y'all my arm was off that day...

WOODY. Off to where?

KING. Why you didn't tell us? We coulda helped you find it.

ELZIE. Kiss my ass.

JIMMY. *(Giggling.)* Kiss his asssss –

KING. Learn to pitch.

UMPIRE. *(Offstage.)* STRIKE TWO!

ELZIE. All I know is, next to Jackie, I'm the best damned player in the world.

> *(While they talk,* **DRUNK WILLIE** *does a slow stroll downstage of the* **PLAYERS** *to get his bat and walk toward the field.)*

TONI. Satchel's the best player in the world.

> *(Beat.)*

I told you guys how I got hit off him in –

ALL. *(Shutting her down.)* YES!!

TONI. *(Undeterred.)* Also Elzie, ain't nobody, other than Satchel, the best player in the world.

> *(Beat.)*

And even Satchel probably can't be the best in the world because you can't know all the players in the world. So how you can know who's best.

WOODY. Can someone shut her up?

> *(Crack of the bat.* **STRETCH** *has hit a single. The* **TEAM** *cheers!)*

JIMMY. See we still in it!

WOODY. Shut up Jimmy.

> *(Beat.)*

WE still in it!

TONI. Yeah Elzie, maybe you better than Jackie next to Jackie, but I don't think you should say you better than everybody...that's exaggerating.

KING. Toni – that literalistness...that can be wearing.

ELZIE. Well I like it in her. 'Cause I like you Toni Stone.

TONI. *(Flattered, not flirtatious.)* You like me Elzie?

ELZIE. I wouldn't throw you outta my bed for eating crackers.

> *(Crack of the bat. **DRUNK WILLIE** gets a hit.)*

SPEC. Hot Damn!!

TONI. *(To **KING**.)* Crackers in a bed?

WOODY. That's crazy that drunk mothafucka can always get a piece.

TONI. *(To **JIMMY**.)* Crackers?

ELZIE. That's more than a piece, that's a run.

> *(He stands. He's up soon. **STRETCH** returns, triumphant. **TONI** ponders as the **PLAYERS** celebrate **STRETCH**'s return.)*

TONI. Why would I eat crackers in your bed? Why would anyone eat crackers in a bed? They are very messy.

ELZIE. *(Affectionately.)* Silly.

> *(He exits with his bat.)*

SPEC. *(To no one in particular.)* "One ever feels his twoness – an American, a Negro." – W.E.B. Du Bois. *The Souls of Black Folk.*

UMPIRE. *(Offstage.)* STRIKE ONE!

KING. You know what's gone happen if they start lettin' some real players up in there...they's either gone have to make it illegal for a Negro man to touch a bat, or they's gone look up and the whole League's colored.

> *(Crack of the bat. **ELZIE**'s made contact. They watch it go up and foul.)*

UMPIRE. *(Offstage.)* FOUL!

TONI. Jackie ain't have an easy road, and ain't gon' get easier.

WOODY. Always actin' like you know something.

UMPIRE. *(Offstage.)* STRIKE THREE!

WOODY. DAMN!!

> **(ELZIE**'s *out. The game's lost. They pack up their equipment.)*

KING. Well, that's it...back to the fuckin' bus.

TONI. How I ain't gone know how he feel?

KING. He who?

ELZIE. She back on Jackie Robinson?

TONI. *(Ignoring him.)* You know them White folks what supposed to be on his team hatin' on him.

WOODY. Ain' nobody hatin' on you Toni.

KING. You hate on her when you feel like it, jess don't call her a nigger.

WOODY. I'll call her a nigger if she want.

ELZIE. Woody!

WOODY. Don't strike out and then Woody me.

TONI. [I'm] Jess saying he's got a hard road ahead of him.

KING. Hard all the way to the bank.

> *(Beat.)*

Stretch, shape these assholes up, I'm tired of losing.

JIMMY. Hey he *(Referring to **KING**.)* struck out, too.

ELZIE. Why you talkin'?

KING. Fool.

STRETCH. Shake it off. We got a game starts in three hours in a town four hours away. Jimmy, go wake up Drunk Willie on second, tell him game's over.

> *(They groan, hurry it up.)*

WOODY. Mothafucka's always asleep on second.

STRETCH. Why you gotta swear about it?

SPEC. Do you all know what the origin of "mothafucka" is?

WOODY. I'm guessing yo mama.

SPEC. They'd make a slave boy climb on his own mama to make a baby to sell. Bad etymology. Word I stay away from.

TONI. Why would I wanna know that Spec? That can only make me feel bad.

WOODY. Well, that mothafucka better do a good job in the majors, or he'll be makin' all you mothafuckas look like mothafuckas –

  (Beat.)

Mothafucka.

  *(**TONI** and **KING** are last to go.)*

KING. Was you expecting all this "glamorousness" back when you was a little girl dreaming about the Negroes?

TONI. *(Sincere.)* Yes.

  (Beat.)

(To audience as she crosses into Jack's.) I was expecting glamorousness, even back when I was talkin' with Alberga, wishing I was playing in the Negro Leagues.

  (In Jack's. It's another day.)

*(To **ALBERGA**.)* All I know Aury is if I don't get into the Negroes, I like to lose my mind. All those little towns I pick up games in, maybe they could have *real* teams if they'd just keep the fields up. I know it's just a soybean field behind a barn, but still, smooth that shit out. Bushes growing in the outfield, like to break your ankle on a mole hill.

ALBERGA. You played a good game today anyway.

TONI. How you know I was playing? I didn't even know 'til that team's poor excuse for a coach called me this morning and asked me to cover.

ALBERGA. I know things.

  *(**TONI** takes it in, pleased.)*

TONI. Don't you think that skinny-ass pitcher they had just needed to hold back? He was wantin' it too much. Too aggressive, can get you ahead of the game, then you all off, for the rest of the night.

ALBERGA. Sometime aggressive just gets you what you want.

TONI. No. I jess sayin', I would'na got a hit off him if he sit back and trust the game. Gotta feel the game and let it tell you. I see these boys, they all in a rush to be ahead... if they'd jess breathe an' find their rhythm the strike zone would find them, the bat'll land where it's s'posed to, if you let *it* tell *you*, but they can't feel it, 'cause they can't slow down to hear it. When you hit it right, feels almost like you didn't hit it at all, like a breath, smooth and easy, when you put it in the right place.

ALBERGA. Toni. You don't even know.

TONI. Oh, I know things Alberga.

ALBERGA. I like you.

TONI. I like you too. You know that. We wouldn't be up in here, talkin' 'til all hours of the night all the time, if I didn't.

ALBERGA. No Toni. I like you.

TONI. Awright.

(*Beat. Finally really hearing him.*)

You tryin' to tell me somethin' I don't understand?

ALBERGA. That's what I'm sayin'.

TONI. You talking sweet to me?

ALBERGA. Yes.

TONI. You ain't talkin' sweet to me. Nobody talks sweet to me.

ALBERGA. Why?

TONI. 'Cause I don't talk sweet. We talk 'bout the game. That's what you an' me do.

ALBERGA. It's the same thing. If you talkin' with your heart.

TONI. I know this girl once. She real pretty. She talk 'bout boys all the time...an' I don't know what she sayin'...

ALBERGA. I ain't a boy Toni. I'm a man. And you can listen to me same way you listen to the game. I'm trying to tell you –

TONI. Stop. I don' like it. I like how we talk now. How we friends now. I don' understand it an' I don' like it an' I hope you will stop this. 'Cause I don' like it. Make me feel tight in my chest. Make my stomach pull an' my legs all wobbly, an' I don't like it. An' you don' even look like you in your eyes, an' I don't like it.

(She walks away, fuming, circling the bar, muttering.)

Alberga, you know Joe Black went thirty and twelve, had a 3.91 ERA, 222 strikeouts. You know how many games he started?

ALBERGA. No.

TONI. Started sixteen. Pitched four shutouts, twenty-five saves, sixty-one base-on-balls, only nine wild pitches. I gotta... I'm just gonna...

*(She moves away from **ALBERGA**, into the dugout.)*

*(**PLAYERS** are spread across the back in the stands. Each has "turned White." They are the **HECKLERS**.)*

(To audience.) New day, new game, we're back with my Clowns. Bottom of the ninth... I just got my third single off some greasy-haired, skinny-ass White boy.

HECKLER 1. Nigga Bitch Jigaboo need to go back to Africa!

TONI. Back in some bumfuck-somewhere-where-they-wouldn't-let-us-sleep town.

HECKLER 2. Why you don't use those big lips to catch the ball!!

TONI. We're ahead: eleven to seven. Don't know if I told you 'bout exhibition games.

HECKLER 3. Goddamn porch monkey clowns give baseball a bad name!

TONI. Did I tell you about exhibition games? Owners'd schedule us on a game opposite a White team. We was to give a show, make 'em look good, let 'em win, and get a cut. But sometimes you just don't have the lose in you.

HECKLER 4. That's that Nigger what tried to brush Billy off the plate... TRY THAT AGAIN NIGGER!

TONI. I'ma tell you exactly how this 'bout to go down Jimmy.

JIMMY. Why now?

HECKLER 5. GODDAMNED BANGY-LIPPED, PORCH MONKEY, COON, NIGGER...!!

> (*JIMMY's terrified.* **TONI,** *seemingly oblivious.*)

TONI. Good a time as any.

HECKLER 1. Ain't no bushbaby whippin' us in our own town!

JIMMY. I don't like this Toni.

TONI. Pay attention, I'm trying to school you. First thing you need to know, everyone has a hole in his swing. See, this batter, he's in trouble, so he'll reach for anything what comes from the left. Other thing is, he always lets the first pitch go, wants to test out the pitcher's arm. Elzie knows this, so he's gonna pitch it fast down the middle.

UMPIRE. (*Offstage.*) STRIKE ONE!

HECKLER 4. (*Shouting.*) Fuckin' bushbaby no 'count nigga!

> (*JIMMY eyes the crowd, terrified.*)

JIMMY. Toni.

TONI. Jimmy, eyes on the game. Now, to set him up, Elzie's gonna throw another fastball, in and off the plate, maybe even brush him back.

JIMMY. (*Terrified.*) Why?

TONI. To get in his head.

UMPIRE. (*Offstage.*) BALL!

HECKLER 3. (*Shouting.*) NIGGER CAN'T THROW!

JIMMY. (*Near panic.*) I thought Stretch said we was takin' a fall?

TONI. We was. But see how Stretch just touched his cap, spit to the left. That means we ain't.

JIMMY. Why?

TONI. 'Cause sometimes they push you a little too far and you gotta punish some White boys that day. Understand Jimmy, [the] game's like chess. Anyone can hit hard, run fast, but you get in the heads of your opponent, that's the money.

>   (*Beat.*)

Now Elzie'll give him another, but this one will go low right over the plate. So Jimmy, if he gets him out, and he will, we gotta run to the bus before they even call it or we gonna get pummeled by these crackers.

UMPIRE. (*Offstage.*) STRIKE TWO!

HECKLER 2. Nigga-lovin' umpire needs glasses.

TONI. You okay Jimmy? You look sick.

JIMMY. I feel sick. You ain't scared?

TONI. 'Course. That's why we gonna run. Pay attention or you miss what I'm trying to show you. You see Elzie's got him scared of his own weakness now, and that's where Elzie wants him. You breathin' Jimmy? Watch. He'll swing at anything. Most likely Elzie'll give him a low and away curveball...he'll pop it up into an easy can of corn up the middle. (*The crack of the bat.*) This's it! Woody's got it.

>   (*They watch the ball go up, up, and:*)

Now Jimmy RUN.

>   (*The **PLAYERS** jump into action, barely time to grab their things. **TONI**'s completely still in the middle of it.*)

UMPIRE. (*Offstage.*) THAT'S THREE!

JIMMY. How'd you do that?

TONI. (*As much for herself as for **JIMMY**.*) It's a special kind of smart.

>   (*The **HECKLERS** turn back into **PLAYERS**, frantically grabbing equipment, building, and getting into the bus. All while **TONI** excitedly addresses the audience:*)

I LOVE RUNNING FOR THE BUS!! Soon as Stretch gives us the sign, boys on the bench run and start pushing the bus, get us as far way as possible so crowd

can't hear us. Woody's on second, he's a sure catch, so
he'll fall back, rest of the field runs, and before the ball's
even hit his glove, we gun the engine, pray it starts, and
soon as Woody's on, we gon' 'fore the White boys know
what happened.

>   (**WOODY** *jumps into the bus last. Lights*
>   *change.*)

Shoot. I ain't told you 'bout the bus.

(*To* **ALBERGA**.) Alberga, I ain't told them about the bus.
How you let me not tell them about the bus?

>   (**ALBERGA** *shrugs. Beat.* **TONI** *moves to the bus.*)

(*To audience.*) This the bus.

>   (*She sits.*)

This where we live late March pretty much through
October.

>   (*Beat.*)

We drive 'til Stretch can't keep his eyes open. So three-
o-clock in the morning, we pull into this podunk hotel,
'bout ten miles from this podunk town we barnstorm
every year, an' ain't never had a problem gettin' rooms
on the sly. Stretch pays off the manager, they bring us
in, round through the kitchen an' put us up in a coupla
rooms what used to be for the cooks. Only this time,
some mad-at-his-life, snaggletooth honky tell us they
don't take niggers up in there. Stretch's thinkin' real
hard 'bout whether he feel like pushin' back on it. But
Stretch sees the same thing I'm seeing, something in
this greasy man's eyes what looks like envy, 'cause he
ain't never got to do what he wanted to do with his life
maybe, and here we are, Niggras getting paid to play
ball. Or maybe he just don't like Niggras, 'cause his
daddy didn't, 'cause his granddaddy didn't have enough
money to buy Niggras. See how I go off. I was tryin' to
tell y'all 'bout something.

ALBERGA. The bus Toni.

TONI. *(To* **ALBERGA.***)* Yes. Thank you.

(To audience.) So, we cain't get off the bus and have to bag back to a town where Stretch thought we might find beds.

> *(The lights go low, all's silent, the* **PLAYERS** *sleep soundly.* **TONI** *walks to the front of the bus, sits on the floor next to* **STRETCH.** *They sit in silence. From time to time headlights zoom past.)*

STRETCH. You can sleep, I'm good.

TONI. I know you alright, just keepin' you company.

> *(Pause.* **STRETCH** *works hard to stay awake.)*

You know Dizzy Dismukes bats right, throws right, started 946 games, only nine errors pretty much ever. Frank Duncan .217 average.

(To wake **STRETCH** *up.)* Stretch, you know Frank's going on now fifteen years with the Monarchs. Bats right, throws right...

Bubbles Anderson, bats right, throws right, batting average –

STRETCH. Toni, I know you mean well, but that thing you like to do there, that's like to make me shoot myself in the head.

TONI. I'm sorry.

> *(More driving.* **STRETCH***'s head's starting to loll.)*

Why you let Woody disrespect you all the time?

STRETCH. That's just what Woody needs to do.

TONI. I wish sometimes you'd tell him to go to [hell] –

STRETCH. Tell him to go where?

TONI. I don't understand why a person would want to work so hard to be an asshole.

STRETCH. You don't know his story.

TONI. We all got stories. Don't have to be bitter 'bout it every second every day.

STRETCH. Why wouldn't he be bitter? He got cheated by the Major Leagues because he didn't have Jackie's "disposition." Woody's got so much talent, but this is the best he's ever gone do.

TONI. We all got talents.

STRETCH. Not like that… You know that.

>   *(Beat.)*

We here. Wake up y'all so you can go to sleep proper.

TONI. *(To* **STRETCH**.*)* Where we at?

>   *(The bus stops. The* **PLAYERS** *shove past* **TONI**, *finding places on the set to sleep.)*

WOODY. Madam Mamie's Gentleman's Club.

TONI. A club?

STRETCH. More like a hotel.

TONI. For men?

WOODY. Jesus Christ.

TONI. Then where do I sleep?

STRETCH. The ladies will take care of you.

TONI. What ladies?

WOODY. *(Brushing past her on his way off the bus.)* Damn Toni. Hoes. Hookers. Prostitutes. Whores. Women of the Night. Strumpets. Harlots. Tarts…

TONI. *(To audience.)* Mama always said I'd end up here if I didn't get a respectable job.

>   *(A* **PLAYER** *becomes* **MILLIE**, *and with* **TONI** *creates her playing space.)*
>
>   *(Note: There is no exaggerated affect in the playing of women. The portrayal is sincere, respectful, and not overplayed. The costume is the removal of a hat, and perhaps the donning of one accessory [a woman's hat, scarf, gloves, purse, etc.]. As the play progresses, Millie's outfit might become a bit more elaborate – but we should not be left with the impression that Millie's character is a man "cross-dressing.")*

MILLIE. You think you'll be alright?

TONI. *(To audience.)* I told you we was gon' meet her.

> *(Beat.)*

This Millie.

MILLIE. You think you'll be alright?

TONI. I'm just glad for the bed. The boys all out sleepin' on that cold bus...

MILLIE. Naw they ain't. Don't fool yourself.

> *(**TONI**'s a little embarrassed.)*

But you can tell yourself that if it suits you.

TONI. I got no reason to judge these men. I suppose we all need comfort. What's your name?

MILLIE. Millie. Just call me Millie like everyone else. These sheets here clean. So you ain't gots to worry –

TONI. Why I be worried?

MILLIE. Well, they clean.

TONI. Thank you Miss Millie.

> *(Beat.)*

Where you gone sleep?

MILLIE. I got work to do.

> *(Beat.)*

There's a washbasin there...put fresh water in it for you. Cup in the cabinet there.

> *(Beat.)*

You hungry? Need somethin' to drink 'sides water?

TONI. No, thank you. You're takin' good care of me.

MILLIE. We don't get famous people up in here much.

TONI. Stop it now. *(But she's pleased.)* I jess play ball.

MILLIE. For all us.

> *(Beat.)*

TONI. Then tha's nice.

> *(Beat.)*

I'm sure you're good at...what you do...too.

(Beat.)

TONI. Where you from?

MILLIE. Roun' 'bout here, there.

(Looking at **TONI**'*s unstraightened hair.)* Y'all catch a rainstorm or two back on the road?

TONI. No...weather's been pretty good.

MILLIE. Well. You wan' I do sumpin' whiff that hair of yours?

TONI. That's nice. No, thank you.

MILLIE. No. You *wan'* I do sumpin' whiff that hair.

TONI. I wear a cap most of the time.

MILLIE. I don' wan' hurt your feelings, but I think it won't hurt you to keep that head lookin' a little more like sumpin'.

> **(MILLIE** *moves to a chair. She invites* **TONI** *to sit on the floor between her legs.)*

A hard-press'll fix you up very nice. Then alls you got to do is put a little grease on it, a few pin curls, and wrap it all up in a silk scarf at night.

TONI. I don't have –

MILLIE. I'll give you a couple of mine.

> *(She works on* **TONI** *with the hot comb.)*

TONI. Thank you.

> *(Beat.)*

My family owned a beauty shop.

MILLIE. [Get the fuck out.] You jess get outta here. An' you didn't learn nothin'?

TONI. You didn't have to say it like that. It just always felt like I could be doin' anything else time I sat in that seat all day. Felt like punishment. And, I didn't like that Negroes weren't allowed in our shop. We had a few wealthy Negroes we'd take in the back, but it always made me feel sick to have to go round to the back and open the door for the ladies what sat in the front row of the church and had better clothes and manners than the White people gettin' fixed up in the front.

MILLIE. You ain't gone believe me, but the Mayor came up here once, asked Miss Mamie would she make this house "Whites only." Ms. Mamie told him, and not so politely, that he had two choices. Could shut her down, or could explain to the good gentlemen, including the mayors of the three or four towns what we service, that they'll have to go two hours out to St. Louis if they was wantin' some professional pussy. Then reminded him that some of the women what work here clean house for those gentlemen and so have the ears of their wives.

(*Beat.*)

So this here what they call an integrated place of business. So, 'bout this hair. (*Adjusting towel.*) Here, do this.

(*She has* **TONI** *hold her ear down*)

TONI. Alright.

MILLIE. Thank you.

(*Beat.*)

Put that head down. Lord this kitchen's nappy.

TONI. You wan' I give you a lil money. No disrespect intended. But you mind I give you a little money?

MILLIE. Naw girl. I don't get much chance to give folks comfort jess because it's what's folks s'posed to do for each other. This gon' be nice. You wait, you'll see, people treat you a lot better when your hair looks right.

TONI. Thank you, Miss Millie.

MILLIE. Please, call me Millie, Miss Toni.

TONI. (*To audience.*) Millie'd put me up whenever we wasn't more than two counties away. The ladies would even send a car for me sometimes. And my boys on the team, what can pay, could stay there too. Me and Spec, we always stay for free.

SPEC. (*Quick, to audience and* **TONI**.) Work that out.

TONI. All up and down our route there's places where the working girls would take me in. So now I think you've

met everyone. Alberga, Syd, my boys, and Millie – my
first female friend.

(She moves to **ALBERGA**, in Jack's.)

ALBERGA. Friends are important.

(Beat.)

Your glass is empty.

TONI. Yes. It is.

ALBERGA. Why don't you do a little Charleston Slide with
me then? Band's nice tonight.

TONI. I don't dance. Besides, you aren't afraid people will
think you funny? You know, a little pansy, bein' with
a girl who always dresses like a man and looks like a
twelve-year-old boy?

ALBERGA. You're a grown-ass woman, Toni Stone.

TONI. Thirty-three.

MILLIE. Lord, Tony! Don't tell a man your age!

TONI. I tell coaches I'm twenty-three...

ALBERGA. I'm sixty-eight. Tell women I'm forty-seven.

TONI. Why would you do that?

ALBERGA. (Amused.) It doesn't matter. I don't know what
people are looking at if they look at you and see boy. I
only see woman.

MILLIE. He's good.

TONI. (To **MILLIE**.) Since you aren't here right now, could
you be quiet please?

(**MILLIE**'s light goes out.)

I'm not good at these things Alberga.

(Pulling back.) Other day this girl who works behind
the counter was talkin' sweet to me...and just like with
you...I didn't know it...but when she explained it to
me, it didn't make me feel nothin' but maybe a little
flattered.

ALBERGA. All of that is arbitrary. You and I have all of the
time in the world to work all of this out.

TONI. I do like the way you speak Aury.

> (**ALBERGA** *moves in, gingerly, for a kiss.* **TONI**
> *pulls back a little, instinctively.*)

ALBERGA. Just make like you the bat and I'm a ball comin'
at it slow.

> (**TONI** *leans into the kiss. It is sweet, tentative,*
> *and short.*)

TONI. Buck Leonard –

ALBERGA. Bats left, throws left...

TONI. How you –

ALBERGA. I know things too sometimes.

TONI. Do you know how many hits he scored last season?

ALBERGA. *(Accepting.)* No Toni, how many?

TONI. Sixty, double that if you add in barnstorming and
exhibition games.

ALBERGA. So again... *(Gesturing to glass.)* What'll you have?

TONI. Just 'cause I let you kiss me doesn't mean I can't get
my own drinks.

MILLIE. Good Lord Toni, the man jess wants to take care of
you a little.

TONI. Then he needs to say what he means. And I take care
of myself just fine.

> *(Beat.)*

(To **ALBERGA.**) Fine then. You may buy me a drink if
you like. Because I know that is important to you.
But, don't think just because I allow you to refresh my
beverage from time to time I can't take care of myself.
That's what I do. I take care of myself.

> (**PLAYERS** *begin to transform the stage into a*
> *steel mill.*)

(To audience.) Always was able to find ways to take
care of myself. Even once I was playing for the Clowns,
money was tight and we all still had to find ways to
scrape through during the off-season.

> (**PLAYERS**, *now* **FACTORY WORKERS**, *wear catchers'
> masks like protective gear for welding.*)
>
> (*Several weld, sending sparks flying. Others
> work, crossing in front and behind, carrying
> "beams," etc. during the following.*)

Last year, I showed up for a job at the steel mill...

> (*The "White"* **SUPERVISOR** *looks at his clipboard.*)

SUPERVISOR. (*Perplexed.*) Toni Stone?

> (*Beat.*)

You're colored?

> (**TONI** *shrugs.*)

AND you're a girl?

TONI. It's Toni with an "I" at the end. If it had a "y" then I'd
be a man. I wasn't tryin' to lie.

SUPERVISOR. Can you weld?

> (*Beat.*)

TONI. Is coffee hot?

SUPERVISOR. Can you weld?

TONI. Hell yeah, I know how to weld. Best welder other
side of the Mississippi.

ALBERGA. (*Impressed.*) That doesn't surprise me.

TONI. (*To* **ALBERGA.**) I don't know a blowtorch from a toaster.
(*To* **MILLIE.**) But I figured out how to put down my mask
and aim the thing at the steel.
(*To audience.*) Well, let's just say...the fire came out...
but the sparks didn't fly...just melted shit that wasn't
s'posed to be melted. Miracle I didn't set myself on fire.

> (*The* **SUPERVISOR** *grabs her by the scruff of her
> neck and starts to walk her out.*)

SUPERVISOR. Like hell you know how to weld! You can't
lie about this kind of thing. What's wrong with you?
Could've burned us all up.

TONI. I didn't lie. I told you I'm the best *other* side of the Mississippi. On the *other* side we do it different.

(*The* SUPERVISOR *appreciates this, despite himself.*)

Listen, (*Pulling a piece of newspaper from her pocket.*) look that's me... (*Striking a baseball card pose.*) I'm famous...if you know baseball, if you know Negro baseball, I'm the girl that plays with the big boys. You want me to work for you.

I'll work hard, I'll get you all tickets, hell, I'll introduce you to Hank Aaron. Does your son like baseball?

SUPERVISOR. Fine. Can you drive?

TONI. Best driver other side the Mississippi.

(*She moves into* MILLIE's *room as though she'd been telling her the story all along.*)

That was if he was talkin' 'bout driving a fastball hard and low and straight up the middle. But I didn't run over nothin' or kill no one, so I kept that job long enough to get me to the season.

MILLIE. I got a regular job once, it didn't work out too good for me though.

TONI. What they found out you were working here and let you go?

MILLIE. No. I was cleaning at the five and dime a few towns over. Dusting, mopping, cleaning the counters. Sometimes the manager made me give him a blowy in the stock closet.

TONI. Ohhh Millie, I'm sorry...

MILLIE. Naw, that wasn't the problem. Problem was they wanted me to clean the bathrooms. Getting on your knees and wiping White people's piss off the floor, that's dirty and degrading work, I had to quit.

TONI. You never wanted to do some other thing?

MILLIE. What I gone do Toni?

TONI. A person can do anything they want if they work real hard.

MILLIE. That's what it seem to you the world looks like?

TONI. Everyone always told me I can't do this or that and I did anyway.

MILLIE. Who was telling you what you could, couldn't do?

TONI. Everybody.

MILLIE. You up there in your nice house, with your nice things, your mama'n'daddy, them teachers and preachers and what not, what cared one way or another what you did. Even if they was saying don't do this or that. That's a whole 'nother kind of what you can't do. So be careful 'bout telling people how it all come out alright if you just work hard.

TONI. Seems like I just made you mad.

MILLIE. *(Deciding to let it go.)* No sweet Toni, it'd be real hard for you to make me mad. Just want you to watch what you say. Make things a lot easier for you.

(Another day at Jack's.)

TONI. Alberga, what if they said to you, "You can't do a thing"?

ALBERGA. I just always knew I could do whatever I want.

TONI. Well, I've been workin' real hard to do whatever I want.

*(She observes her **MOTHER** on the porch.)*

MOTHER. Marcenia, baseball is so dirty, and the boys spit, and are always touching their *(Beat.)* nethers. Perhaps you could join the team with those people who run.

TONI. *(To audience)* I joined the track team. Came in second fastest in my division.

*(A **PLAYER** hands **TONI** a trophy, which she walks over and hands to her **MOTHER**, still addressing the audience.)*

*(To **ALBERGA**.)* Yeah, when you a girl, jus' soon as they tell you you cain't, all you can do is feel bad about yourself...

MOTHER. Marcenia, we've signed you up for figure skating. Every Monday, Wednesday, and Friday. See that you go, and get there on time.

TONI. *(To* **MOTHER.***)* But how I'm gonna tell the boys, can't practice Monday, Wednesdays and Fridays, 'cause I hafta skate around in a skirt?

(To **ALBERGA.***)* I put on that stupid skirt and I placed first in state. Excuse me.

>   *(She returns to her* **MOTHER** *and hands her trophies, and plaques, and her skates.)*

(To **MOTHER.***)* So, now may I go play ball?

(To **ALBERGA.***)* Alberga, they tried so hard to tell me I couldn't do even that. It wears on a person.

>   *(Beat.)*

It don't wear on you?

ALBERGA. Naw baby –

TONI. *(To audience and* **MILLIE,** *trying it out, kind of liking it.)* Baby.

ALBERGA. I don't let people tell me what I can't do. I stay too far in front of it to let it wear on me.

TONI. *(To* **MILLIE.***)* Millie, sometimes he says something exactly in the way that I would have said it myself if I had the words.

MILLIE. I know that feeling.

TONI. It confuses me. For someone to be up inside of my thoughts like that.

MILLIE. Feels good, don't it.

>   *(Through the following, lights and sound change until all is quiet and* **TONI** *is in a tight spot.)*

TONI. *(To audience.)* Yesterday, we're down five, bottom of the fourth, and when we're behind is usually when I can go deeper in the game, when everything else clears

away and it's quiet all around and it's just me and the
pitcher and then the ball leaves his hand and the world
falls away more, and it's just me and that ball, and I
know where it's gonna go, and my body knows just
exactly what it needs to do to answer to whatever that
ball's gonna do...and all of a sudden...

ALBERGA. Baby.

> (*Lights and sound restore abruptly, startling*
> **TONI** *out of her reverie.*)

> (**TONI** *swings, misses. Thud of ball hitting*
> *catcher's mitt.*)

UMPIRE. (*Offstage.*) STRIKE ONE!

TONI. Alberga comes into my head.

(*To* **MILLIE.**) What the hell is that anyway, baby? Baby?
I'm a grown woman.

> (*She swings and misses.*)

UMPIRE. (*Offstage.*) STRIKE TWO!

TONI. Dammit.

MILLIE. You don't like it 'cause it feels good when he says it.

ALBERGA. Stay in front of it baby and it won't wear on you.

> (**TONI** *doesn't swing. Sound of ball swishing*
> *by, hitting catcher's mitt.*)

TONI. Strike three, right.

UMPIRE. (*Offstage.*) STRIKE THREE!

TONI. Like people can't count to three... Gotta yell strike
three like you happy 'bout it. And 'sides, that one was
low and outside. Umpire's blind today, sun in my eyes...
And another thing...

> (*She starts for Jack's.*)

MILLIE. Ohhh Toni, you love him.

TONI. I don't have time for that Millie.

MILLIE. Can't help that.

TONI. See if I can't.

(In Jack's.)

ALBERGA. Toni, if someone asked you to marry him, would you consider it?

TONI. It would depend on who the person is.

MILLIE. That ain't cute Toni.

TONI. What?

MILLIE. You know what that man is trying to say.

TONI. I don't want to get married Millie.

MILLIE. He's got a job and a house and seem to genuinely like you.

TONI. *(To* **MILLIE**.*)* Even if I did get married, I'm the only person I would belong to.

MILLIE. Keep telling yourself that.

ALBERGA. Now see, you're just trying to make this difficult.

MILLIE. It do seem like that.

TONI. It is difficult.

ALBERGA. I love you.

> *(Beat.* **TONI** *appreciates that he's said it but doesn't respond.)*

MILLIE. Toni!

ALBERGA. I said I love you, Toni, you need to say something back.

TONI. If you ate some crackers in my bed I would not make you have to get out of it.

> *(Beat.)*

I told you about John Wesley Donaldson, went sixteen and ten, 1.6 ERA, started forty-one games, threw only one wild pitch in six years –

ALBERGA. You got to stop that.

TONI. I gotta go.

> *(***ALBERGA***'s light goes out.)*

(To audience.) See how the reach keeps changing, and how that thing between the reach and the ball...steady wants to move around on you.

(Beat, beat.)

(**TONI** *makes her way to dugout.*)

TONI. Cool Papa Bell – center field, switch-hitter. Seventy-three –

STRETCH. Toni. Toni, you listenin' to me?

TONI. ...Seventy-three home runs, eight-time All Star, life average – 337.

STRETCH. Where you at today Toni?

TONI. *(To audience.)* Deep into the season sometimes I don't even know myself.

WOODY. Always muttering to herself – it's unnerving.

ELZIE. How you gon' talk Woody? [You] Touch your nose, turn round three times, spit left, spit right, can't nobody say boo to you top of the fifth.

KING. That's some retard shit if I ever seen it.

ELZIE. So what it matter to you Toni says a couple of words to herself sometime.

SPEC. Retard...not a good word. Y'all want to know the etymology of retard?

ALL. NO!

STRETCH. All y'all just salty 'cause we goin' into the fifth down.

TONI. *(To audience.)* In the Negroes, top of the fifth's coonin' time. And Stretch right...

STRETCH. We can have fun, or we can look like we sad 'cause the White folks made us do it. Everyone gets a bad show, and then who cares who wins. Please, can we just let silly, be silly today.

KING. Ain't feeling much like clowning today Toni.

TONI. I could see it in his eyes before he said it. Sometimes you just wanna leave your silly on the bus where *we* know it's silly, not stupidness.

   (To **KING**.*)* King, why don't you take it easy and we'll take the eyes off you for a while. Right, Woody?

WOODY. Yep.

KING. You do that for me?

> (**SPEC** *puts his book down and starts to juggle.*)

TONI. How we not do that for you?

(To audience.) King know I don' mind, long as Coach puttin' me in.

> *(Music plays.* The **PLAYERS** *get up to do acrobatics, clown around. After a point, the music becomes just a little bit darker.* **TONI***'s becoming agitated watching it.)*

> *(The "show" that started like the one we saw at the top of the play is morphing into something horrific.)*

> *(***TONI*** *walks down center as the movement continues at a fevered pitch, but in silence, punctuated only by the percussive sounds of their physical exertions.)*

Our people always did have a way of turning what matters into something beautiful that touches the soul. We call that laughter and they call that clowning. But you know they know. They know it's powerful so's they come back for more of it. But they also know they can't do it... Never mind catch a pop an' flip back an' throw it in for the double play.

> *(The **PLAYERS** stop, one at a time, looking at the audience as* **TONI** *talks. They breathe heavily from the exertion.)*

White people think if it's fun an' have a certain elegance it ain't serious. But they know. Everyone knows they can't turn what's practical into something more, the Charleston Slide, the Mississippi slow grind, or the art of making a skill pretty.

---

*A license to produce *Toni Stone* does not include a performance license for any third-party or copyrighted music. Licensees should create an original composition or use music in the public domain. For further information, please see Music Use Note on page 3.

TONI. So they laugh and give us a little bit of money so they keep laughing, but they know it's powerful and they know that we know what they doin' to us while we still steady makin' 'em laugh.

>*(All of the **PLAYERS** stand, still looking at the audience for a beat, then peel off one or two at a time, exiting in different directions. **TONI** leaves the stage last. Stadium lights flash brightly and go dark.)*

ACT II

(TONI and KING sit on the lip of the stage. They look at the audience for a while...settling in.)

KING. Possible we scared them a little bottom of the first.

TONI. King, I ever told you I got a hit off Satchel Paige in –

KING. Yes.

TONI. Told you 'bout the time when –?

KING. Several times.

TONI. What about –

KING. Yessiree.

(Beat.)

(TONI looks defeated. KING takes pity on her.)

Toni. Why don't you tell me 'bout Gabby Street...

(Beat.)

Again.

TONI. *(Thrilled.)* Gabby and the Washington Monument? Gabby and the shoes? Gabby and the earthquake? Gabby and the World Series in...

(KING just looks at her, amused exasperation.)

The glove.

KING. *(To audience.)* Y'all wanna know about Gabby Street. And the glove?

(Beat.)

TONI. *(To audience.)* Don't be scared – it's a good story. Gabby and the Glove.

(The TEAM comes in, transforms the stage into a baseball field of Toni's youth.)

(**KING** *silently mouths the first few words of this along with* **TONI**. *She's told it, exactly like this, a million times.*)

TONI. Every summer, when I was a girl, Coach Gabby Street ran a baseball club for the most talented –

KING. Or richest...

TONI. White boys in the Twin Cities. Gabby was a famous catcher, then a famous coach in the Majors for over twenty years. He had stories on top of stories about his courageous exploits on and off the field. When he was twenty-four his team had a game in San Francisco when the big earthquake came. It swallowed the hotel they were staying in, and he was the one that got away, with nothing but his life and his britches. And then –

KING. Toni.

TONI. The Glove...

KING. Yes.

TONI. Okay.

(*Beat.*)

All I wanted to do is know half as much as Coach Gabby did. So, I went on down to Lexington Park where Gabby held court with the White boys.

(*Beat.*)

I'm a little girl.

(*The* **PLAYERS** *become* **WHITE BOYS**. *They stand around* **COACH GABBY STREET**, *listening to him pontificate about the finer points of the game.* **TONI**, *a girl now, stands at the periphery.*)

COACH GABBY. People want the game to be about the pitch. Yeah Buster, you're a good pitcher. We got that, we appreciate that...but boys, I've told you and I've told you...you gotta put in those hours of batting practice. Put out your hands.

(*The* **BOYS** *hold out their hands, palms up.*)

Soft. Why do I waste my time. You should all have calluses this late into summer. And let me see that bat son.

(He takes a couple of swings.)

This damn bat's too heavy for me. How many times have I told you, you don't get a home run swing off of a bat that's too heavy.

*(**TONI** soaks it in, so lost in the moment that she forgets she's not part of the group.)*

TONI. *(Excitedly, to **COACH GABBY**.)* It's true, Coach. I used to be thinkin' if the bat was heavy I'd get some good momentum on it, and I did, but it didn't put the ball where I wanted it. And, half the time I'd come round too slow and miss it. You get a light bat, you can hook it up a little on a pitch that's almost high, pull the ball, get some spin, and put it right where he's gotta look into the sun...

(Silence.)

COACH GABBY. What are you doing here?

TONI. Listenin'. Learnin'.

(She looks around as though surely he must be speaking to someone behind her.)

COACH GABBY. Well, git.

*(A change in light and a shift of the **BOYS'** positions. It's another day of baseball camp. **TONI** stands to the side, making herself inconspicuous.)*

Billy, you had the opening to take the steal. Good eye. But stupid. Where's your guy on third gonna go if you run and the ball's already three quarters of the way down? You gonna distract the batter off of a really good hit. Sit tight. Wait for your team to be ready. Won't matter if you're safe at second if your teammate's out at home. Jesus Christ, thick as molasses and dumb as my dog's butt. Someone please repeat back to me what I said.

JUNIOR. Dumb as my dog's butt.

TONI. You're saying put the game before yourself.

> (*The* **COACH** *sees her.* **TONI** *gives the wide-eyed,
> "You talkin' to me?" look.*)

COACH GABBY. Girl, didn't I tell you to git?!

TONI. Not today.

COACH GABBY. GIT!!

> (*Another shift. Another day.* **COACH GABBY**
> *simply stops talking and looks at* **TONI**.)

You're back?

TONI. I know how to play.

> (*To one of the* **BOYS**.) Junior, you know me. Tell Coach
> Gabby I can play.

> (**JUNIOR** *averts his eyes.*)

Look Coach, how hard my hands are.

> (*The* **BOYS** *turn their backs.* **COACH GABBY**
> *gives no indication that he's seen her.*)

(*To audience.*) I believe that's when Gabby saw what I
had. Real baseball players, we see one another.

> (*Two of the* **BOYS** *play catch. One of them,
> proudly, over his shoulder to* **COACH GABBY**:)

BOY. Look, Coach Gabby. She's back.

COACH GABBY. Boy, if you have your eyes in the right place
you shouldn't have time to see anything but that ball
comin' at your pea-size head. Turn around and get your
head in the game.

TONI. And if Gabby was in a good mood, he might throw
with me after camp. Somewhere along the way he
forgot I was a girl, and that I was Colored. At the end
of summer he gave me my first real glove. It was old,
but it was well-conditioned and felt right. Like we was
supposed to be together and just came to each other
late.

*(The **WHITE BOYS** and **COACH GABBY** turn into
the **PLAYERS** again and retire to the bus. Some
play cards, some sleep.)*

*(**TONI** joins **ALBERGA** in Jack's.)*

It was years later 'fore I learned Gabby was in the KKK.
I would picture him leaving the field and going home
and putting on a sheet and going out and hanging
someone's daddy or uncle. And it would make me sick
to my stomach.

(Beat.)

I still sleep with that glove. I don't understand how I
can make it separate from Gabby. But I do. It is.

ALBERGA. You don't have to sleep with a glove Toni. Plenty
of things more pleasant to sleep with than a glove.

TONI. *(To **MILLIE**.)* Seem like he make a good point.

MILLIE. I been tellin' you that hardhead.

TONI. *(To audience.)* So, I'm engaged. To a man. To be
married. Mother doesn't know what to do with herself.
She's never been to a game, but spends hours holdin'
lacy white things up next to other lacy white things.
Syd loves it. Has reporters take pictures of me in my
uniform with a veil on my head.

(Beat.)

It's a whole lot happenin' real fast Millie.

*(Light up on **MILLIE**.)*

MILLIE. Ain't things s'posed to be fast in baseball?

*(The **PLAYERS** resume positions from the top
of the play. They spot, freeze in the reach.)*

TONI. *(To **ALBERGA**.)* Did I ever tell them about when I met
Syd?

ALBERGA. Don't know.

TONI. *(To **MILLIE**.)* Millie?

MILLIE. Just tell your story sweetie.

TONI. What I'm trying to work out is somewhere in what's about to happen, and I think it's at the high point of the reach.

>   (**ALBERGA** *watches from Jack's Tavern. Out of the "reach,"* **TONI** *makes the winning catch. The* **PLAYERS** *go crazy. A* **PLAYER** *becomes* **SYD** *again.*)

SYD. You're the girl I hear so much about.

TONI. *(To audience.)* I wasn't a "girl."

>   If I was a girl, I'd have said to you, "I'm a little girl." So instead, "I'm a woman" and this is when I met Syd.

SYD. You're the girl I hear so much about.

TONI. Depends on what you hear about me.

MILLIE. Smart-ass.

SYD. You played a good game today.

TONI. Thank you. I always play hard. You're Mr. Sydney Pollock what owns the Clowns.

SYD. Syd.

TONI. Mr. Pollock.

SYD. You think you can handle a real league?

TONI. Are you offering me a job Mr. Pollock?

SYD. Syd.

TONI. You offering me a job?

SYD. I can give you a tryout in a couple of games.

TONI. I hear you pay pretty good.

SYD. Let's try you out. See how you do.

TONI. But you've seen me play. That's why you're here, right? I'll do a lot better for you if I'm paid what I'm worth. Can't have my head in the game right, if I think I'm always trying out. You saw what I can do. You've got my stats.

>   *(From where she is, to* **ALBERGA**.*)* That's another thing about baseball I like. It is what it is, and it is beautiful.

ALBERGA. It is beautiful.

SYD. I can't play you the whole game. Gotta let the boys get used to playing with a girl. Gotta give our fans a show. Can't have your pride get in the way of how I sell tickets.

TONI. I don't understand.

(*To audience.*) Listen close.

SYD. I may have them slow their pitches, serve 'em up, groove them.

TONI. (*To audience.*) You hear that?

(*To* **SYD.**) Fix my pitches? No.

MILLIE. Sometimes you gotta do whatchu gotta do Toni.

TONI. (*To* **MILLIE.**) How you get in this?

ALBERGA. Ask for six hundred a month.

TONI. (*To* **SYD.**) How's the team gonna respect me?

MILLIE. Gotta find your own respect.

TONI. (*To* **MILLIE.**) I don't remember asking you.

(**MILLIE**'s *light goes off.*)

SYD. Team doesn't have to know. Just the pitchers.

TONI. (*To* **SYD.**) No. I'm not taking rigged pitches. I played 179 games last year, 412 at-bats, .280 average, 150 hits, twenty-two two-baggers, six triples, ninety-eight ribbies, stole eight, thirty walks, four sacs...

ALBERGA. So your pride's greater than your desire to play ball?

TONI. Dammit.

ALBERGA. Ask for six hundred a month.

TONI. (*To* **SYD.**) Six hundred a month then.

SYD. That's more than my high-stat rookies make.

TONI. You ain't makin' your high-stat rookies hit bogus pitches. You saw how I did. Didn't need special treatment.

SYD. It's non-negotiable. This is new territory and I need to insure my investment.

TONI. (*Troubled.*) Six hundred if you're rigging my pitches.

SYD. How you figure?

TONI. If I'm risking my pride and reputation so you can get easy homers, then I need six hundred. That's two-fifty skill, plus two-fifty reputation and pride.

SYD, ALBERGA & MILLIE. That's five hundred.

TONI. *(To* **ALBERGA.***)* I know that.

    (To **SYD.***)* I know that. The last hundred is because you're gonna give me less than I'm asking. So, six hundred.

ALBERGA. That's a very strange negotiating tactic.

TONI. *(Kind of proud and feeling cute.)* It is, isn't it.

SYD. Am I going to regret this?

TONI. I promise that I will be the most steady, hardworking player you've ever signed.

SYD. Two forty-five.

ALBERGA. Three fifty.

TONI. Three fifty.

SYD. Two forty-five.

TONI. *(To* **ALBERGA.***)* That sounds good.

ALBERGA. Three hundred.

TONI. Three hundred.

SYD. If you don't play better than you negotiate they'll be rigged all the time. I'm giving you three hundred. One hundred's for your skill, one hundred's for your pride, and the other hundred's because I was planning on giving you three fifty anyway. *(Offering his hand.)* Deal?

TONI. Deal.

ALBERGA. He's good.

    *(**TONI** and **SYD** shake hands.)*

TONI. One more thing.

ALBERGA. You can't have one more thing after you shake.

MILLIE. You can always have one more thing.

SYD. We shook.

TONI. We can shake again.

(Beat.)

You have to promise that if I field better than thirty percent of your men, you have to call off the fake pitches. Deal.

(She extends her hand.)

SYD. *(Taking it.)* You're an odd duck.

MILLIE. Don't like he called you that.

TONI. So long as I'm an odd duck what plays for the Clowns.

(To audience.) So, you caught that? That other piece of the reach... The piece that makes you do things you never thought you would. Important you caught all that.

*(She makes her way to **ALBERGA** at the bar.)*

*(To **ALBERGA** and audience.)* This how I imagine the talk that Syd had with the other White owners went...

*(The **PLAYERS** have turned into **WHITE OWNERS**. Benches have been stacked, two on each side with the score laid on top to form a conference-room table.)*

SYD. I'm going to need your boys to pitch her cookies. And make them stop brushing her off the plate.

OWNER 1. That's bullshit.

SYD. That's what I need.

OWNER 3. Alright, let me get this straight. You came to us, said, I want you to let me put a girl on my team. You made a decent argument, had your little Jimmy Stewart moment, and we said okay. Now you're asking us to start fixing shit?

SYD. What do we call it when we ask our boys to take a dive for the White teams?

OWNER 1. Let's say my boys do pitch her cookies. How's that gonna set them up to impress scouts?

SYD. So you're trying to lose our best players to the majors?

OWNER 1. No.

SYD. Then give me a better argument.

OWNER 4. It messes with the integrity of the game.

SYD. You make them wear grass skirts and paint their faces.

OWNER 3. It's entertainment. We're trying to fill seats, not have integrity. Your numbers coming up because of this girl Syd?

SYD. By thirty-five percent.

OWNER 4. Thirty-five percent?!

SYD. I'm just asking you to give the crowd a little of what they come for. In truth, my girl can out-hit most of your weakest players, and some of the better ones. But I need to be able to count on it, so the crowds come back. Now don't get me wrong, she's no cupcake. The girl can play.

OWNER 1. Yeah, I've seen her.

OWNER 4. I haven't.

OWNER 3. You need to, 'cause I haven't ever seen anything like it.

OWNER 2. Well I'm out. I won't ask my boys to cheat.

SYD. Those people fillin' your seats, buying your stale peanuts and soft popcorn, aren't comin' here to watch a bunch of assholes hit that girl that even the people in the cheap seats can see plays with her heart. If they wanna see a game, even the Niggras can go to the big parks now. They wanna see a show. They wanna see something spectacular.

OWNER 1. Fine. But you're comin' to my dugout to explain it yourself.

SYD. It's just a conversation between us and the pitchers... we treat it like it's another day, it'll be another day.

> (The **OWNERS** morph into **PLAYERS**. **TONI**'s been up to bat.)

UMPIRE. (Offstage.) STRIKE THREE!

> (**TONI**'s struck out.)

TONI. Dammit all to hell!

(She kicks up dirt, throws her bat down.)

(JIMMY's up. He exits to the field.)

WOODY. How you miss that?

ELZIE. Don't start up with her Woody.

TONI. *(To audience.)* Syd hasn't kept his promise, but I don't swing at bullshit anymore.

UMPIRE. *(Offstage.)* STRIKE ONE!

WOODY. I say Toni, how you miss that?

ELZIE. Woody!

WOODY. Did I say something to you Elzie?
(Getting **TONI**'s *attention.)* Toni.

TONI. I missed it same way you choked top of the second I guess. 'Cept no one 'spects nothin' else from me, you on the other hand, you choke and my fans just know you ain't got no God-given talent, just like we already knew.

WOODY. Don't have to go all sensitive and shit.

UMPIRE. *(Offstage.)* STRIKE TWO!

WOODY. Motherfucker!
(To **TONI**.*)* Damn Toni, I was jess ribbin' you!

TONI. Go to hell Woody!

WOODY. Go home and make some curtains Toni.

UMPIRE. *(Offstage.)* STRIKE THREE!

(JIMMY's struck out. **STRETCH** *grabs his bat and walks onto the field, giving* **JIMMY** *a look that could kill as he passes by.* **JIMMY** *returns to the dugout, defeated.)*

WOODY. *(To* **JIMMY**, *feigned concern.)* You alright?

(Over the course of the scene, **STRETCH**, *unseen by us, swings and misses, hits fouls, lets pitches go by – some good, some bad. He gets out at the end of the scene.)*

(In the dugout, all watch the game intently beyond the fourth wall.)

JIMMY. Yeah.

WOODY. Maybe you should let me look at that bat.

> (*Beat.*)

JIMMY. It's fine Woody.

WOODY. 'Cause I think sumpin' might be wrong witch-yo bat.

ELZIE. (*To* **KING**, *out of earshot of* **JIMMY**.) Aw Lord, here he go…

KING. Someone 'bout to get fucked with…

WOODY. Heard 'bout this whole shipment of bats, what got left on the truck in the winter too long and done got warped from the top down to the handle. You hear about that Spec…

SPEC. Ain'tchu up next Woody?

JIMMY. (*Out, to* **STRETCH**.) Keep your head in the game…he ain't throwin' nothing…

ELZIE. Tell me he didn't just tell Stretch how to play?

TONI. Uh-huh.

JIMMY. Tha's right! Tha's right Stretch. Show 'em what we've got.

ELZIE.	**SPEC**.
Jesus.	Jesus. He wants to make it hard for himself.

WOODY. Hey Jimmy, I know you used to me fuckin' with you boys, but seriously though…you need to take a close look at that bat…keep you hittin' high an' swingin' a bit to the right…ain't no way no one gone get a hit widda warped bat. Right Elzie?

ELZIE. (*Now in on it.*) Aww yeah… I heard 'bout those…they sent a wire round to the White boys 'bout it –

> (*Crack of bat.* **STRETCH** *has gotten a piece. They watch it go up and up, and out.*)

UMPIRE. (*Offstage.*) FOUL BALL!

KING. Then they come an' sell it to our fool owners what don't care how we look out there –

WOODY. You gotta look at the top of it…

(STRETCH has made a strike.)

UMPIRE. *(Offstage.)* STRIKE!

JIMMY. Spec?

> *(SPEC, enjoying despite himself, gives JIMMY
> a shrug.)*

WOODY. See, there a little curve what go in right there in
the middle of the bat. It's your bat. I seen you hit that
ball, you gots a defect what's wrong wiff you today.
Here, let me see it...

> *(JIMMY hands him the bat. WOODY makes a
> big show of looking at it, then gives it back
> to him.)*

Yeah...feel it, right here...see how it have that bump...
Right there, an' if you run your hand down the length
of it, like that...

> *(WOODY helps JIMMY adjust so the bat is held
> between JIMMY's legs.)*

There...see, rub it up an' down there...see there...

JIMMY. *(Clearly relieved.)* I don't know... I think...maybe...

WOODY. Make your hand round, take it all the way down...
you feel it? Gotta do it faster...up and down...there you
feel that?

JIMMY. Yeah...

WOODY. You know what that feel like?

> *(Beat. JIMMY gets what's just happened off of
> the PLAYERS' laughs)*

That you stupid, an' need to figure out how to get a
piece of that ball...or jus' take that bat home an' make
love to it like you doin' now...'cause that seem be all it
good for for you today.

> *(Beat.)*

(As he walks away.) Motherfucker.

> *(Crack of the bat. STRETCH has made contact.
> They watch it go up...it's caught.)*

UMPIRE. *(Offstage.)* YOU'RE OUT!

ELZIE.   **KING.**

Goddammit!   There it is.

> *(**TONI** moves away from the dugout.)*

TONI. *(To audience.)* Wasn't even married yet when Syd comes to me with...

> *(A **PLAYER** turns into **SYD**.)*

SYD. I'm sorry Toni, gotta take you down two dollars a paycheck.

TONI. But I'm your best rookie.

SYD. Now that you're engaged you could up and leave me in a lurch, or worse, get in the family way.

TONI. Been meaning to talk to you too, Syd. I'm still getting bullshit pitches. Puts me in a bad position. You promised that if I...

SYD. Let's stay on track Toni.

TONI. I don't stay on track Syd. That's not something I do. What it matter what you pay me now, even if I did leave later? And I won't.

SYD. I'd have to find another girl. That cost money. All those flyers and posters with your face on 'em, cost money. Maybe I'll get a mascot instead. A team over in Greenville has an elephant that's bringing in fans.

TONI. *(To **ALBERGA**.)* How he gonna say I can be replaced by a reptile?

ALBERGA. Mammal.

TONI. You do see what I'm trying to say Alberga.

SYD. You aren't swinging at half the home run pitches they're giving you anyway.

TONI. I don't have to anymore because I am no longer, no longer –

ALBERGA. Contractually bound.

TONI. Contractually bound.

SYD. There was no contract.

TONI. We shook on it. If I met my stats, no more easy pitches.

SYD. We're done with this Toni.

TONI. *(Frustrated beyond words.)* Syd, if you were not my boss I would say go to hell. But I have been told that that is not a thing you can say to your boss. So I'm not gonna say it.

(**SYD** *exits as* **TONI** *goes to* **MILLIE**.*)*

MILLIE. You didn't say that.

(**TONI** *nods.)*

I'm trying to help your Black ass...but you won't sit on your thoughts. What I keep telling you?

TONI. Watch what I say... But I'm just saying, why Syd think keepin' me on the road like he do, I'd have time to lay on back long enough to get in a family way.

MILLIE. It don't take long Toni.

TONI. Stop all that now.

MILLIE. And it don't have to be on your back.

(Beat.)

But you do have to have relations with the man.

TONI. We jus' engaged. We aren't even married yet.

MILLIE. Of course. 'Cause that's what grown-ass people do. Wait 'til they get married.

(**TONI** *moves to the bus. It's as though she's been there the whole time.* **KING**'s *mid-story.)*

TONI. ...So you come home an' the house all quiet?

WOODY. Jesus King, why you always gotta drag out a story?

ELZIE. You got somewhere you need to be?

KING. I'm jess tryin' to tell you fools what happened. In the 'mount of time you talkin' 'bout how long I'm talkin', we coulda been got to Pittsfield, won the game, and be back on the bus.

TONI. So you come home and...

KING. An' the house all quiet an' dark, an' I hear my old lady scream, "Oh Lord you's 'bout to kill me with that thing..." An' I go runnin' to find her...'cause I thinkin' she need my help... An' it's comin' from the pantry... The pantry of all things... And if it wasn't that boy what brings by the groceries, 'cause her ass too lazy to walk to the corner for a loaf of bread...got my wife bent over, ridin' her like he's gone ride her to Timbuktu an' back... Thing is, I always thought if you was gone see somethin' like that, that rage just supposed to take over an' you see red, no countin' for wachu might do. And I'm standing there, thinkin', "Damn, now I gots to beat this nigga's ass and throw him in the street..." But it's been a long day, and all I wanta do is get my feet soaking in some Epsom salts. And suddenly, that shit seems funny.

SPEC. You full of shit...

KING. Serious, you would too...picture Wilomena's big ol' ass just jiggling an' that skinny kid lookin' like he done found heaven with his britches down at his knees an' his eyes rollin' back...an' he's got his hand up, 'bout to slap it good, an' they see me, an' he just stop...just freeze...like this. *(He gets up, shows it...)* Jus' like this... an' I'm laughin' harder, 'cause you know under the best circumstances when people be goin' at it, it's funny... Thank God we don't be seein' ourselves doin' all that mess 'cause it look stupid...

SPEC. I don't look stupid... Hell, people'd pay to see me do it.

KING. An' I'm laughing so hard I cain't stand up...an' that's scarin' them more...an' she commence to cryin'...loud howls..."Lord Jesus, I don't know what's got into me lately King, must be 'the change' comin' on... I's so sorry..." An' still I cain't stop myself laughing...

TONI. For real King?

KING. Dyin' if I'ma Lyin'. Finally I says, "Boy, pull up them britches an' cover that little thing." Then I say, "Meena... I'ma need you to cook me a meal what's bigger'n Easter, Thanksgiving and Christmas all together." An' the boy's so scared he cain't move, just standin' there eyes bucked out and shakin' an' his pants all down by his ankles now. An' I say, "You wan' I can call over to your mama and ask can you stay for dinner? Meena, here's 'bout to fix me a feast. Today, an every day for the rest of my life." An' he starts to crying, just wailin', they both wailin', an' that's the funniest damn thing I ever seen.

SPEC. At a carnival up in Wisconsin last summer, they paid seventy-five cents to see me do it with a lady with a beard.

> *(Beat, beat, beat.)*

TONI. Did they pay you because she had a beard or because you are short, or because your penis is very long.

> *(Beat.)*

SPEC. Yes.

TONI. *(From bus to MILLIE's area.)* I don't know why that's funny. Why? Why would that be funny Millie? *(Crossing.)* Someone having intercourse with your wife and White people paying to watch a short man copulate with...

MILLIE. What'd I tell you about funny?

TONI. *(Crossing to MILLIE.)* Sometimes things just funny 'cause somebody laughs.

> *(**MILLIE** unwraps a binding...an athletic tape of some sort. As she unwinds it we see that **TONI**'s back is covered in bruises.)*

MILLIE. Oh Toni, this one is shaped like a foot. They kick you?

TONI. It's part of the game Millie, don't worry.

MILLIE. Who did this?

TONI. Some White boy in an exhibition game down in Pittsfield. But they all do it. I play second. All they have to do is slide into me with their feet high. They just want to scare you off the base so they're safe.

MILLIE. There should be a rule.

TONI. There is. No matter.

MILLIE. You ever wonder why there's those of them that hate us?

TONI. All White people hate us.

MILLIE. Men.

TONI. I know lots of men what love women.

MILLIE. I don't know. Sometimes even when they're on top of me, there's part of them want to make me hurt. Maybe for some other woman...like they pay good money could be spent lovin' to be hatin' on me. It's the same things they doin' but like they hate me.

TONI. I don't know 'bout all that.

MILLIE. Well I do. And I know when I see a bruise like this, the bastard what made it felt good when he did. Made his willy stand up just a little when he did that to you.

(Beat.)

Oh my God, is that a rib? That couldn't be right. Alberga see this?

TONI. No. Oh no. I couldn't let him see this.

MILLIE. There's a doctor, come every other night round four to spend time with Valerie, you want I get him to look at you?

TONI. No. When doctors start telling you how bad it is, it starts to feel bad. I don't have time to be out two weeks. I'd lose my mind. And maybe my job.

MILLIE. Now hold still. I just wanna get this cleaned good. And we have to wash those bandages. That's not good for you. Here...

*(She helps **TONI** into a dressing gown. It seems strange somehow. We've never seen **TONI** this uncomfortable. She seemed more covered before the dressing gown went on.)*

Look at you. You know you'd look real pretty if you let yourself. At least, for that old man you got.

TONI. He seem to like me how I am just fine.

MILLIE. You'd be surprised. They very much 'bout what they see. Keep that dressing gown, it suits you.

TONI. Honestly Millie sometimes you sound like my mother.

MILLIE. I'd pay to have her hear you say that.

TONI. It's not funny. You all gotta stop trying to make me into...asking me to be... To act like... They think I'm a girl out there, they ain't gone throw the ball to me. Besides, I can't be ridin' on a bus with a bunch of randy men who got girls like you and girls givin' it away for free...

MILLIE. ...

TONI. Seem like I made you mad.

MILLIE. ...

TONI. Coulda just said thank you for the robe and not wore it?

MILLIE. ...

TONI. I'm sorry.

MILLIE. Honestly Toni, I don't understand why you wanna keep getting hurt playing a children's game with boys.

TONI. What you do hurts too, don't it?

(**MILLIE** *brushes past* **TONI,** *insulted.*)

MILLIE. Alright then, I'm going down to Lenore to get some liniment and a couple of aspirin for you. (*On her way out, considering.*) I'll leave the things outside the door.

TONI. Haven't seen you in a while, I thought... You ain't comin' back?

MILLIE. I'ma stay in Lenore's room with Spec.

TONI. Spec?

MILLIE. Yes. Spec.

(*Beat.*)

And Toni, it do hurt sometimes. Don't be askin' me shit like that again. You might wanna change those sheets.

(*It's late at night. The* **PLAYERS** *on the bus are asleep.* **TONI** *takes the ointment and moves to behind the bus.*)

TONI. Tennessee Joe: lifetime average .400, bats left, throws right, 710 hits, ninety doubles, 110 home runs, 351 RBIs, twenty-eight stolen bases, 136 walks.

    (She removes the robe and bandages, topless,
    her back to the audience. She gingerly puts
    ointment on her wounds. **ELZIE** *happens upon*
    her from upstage, toilet paper in his hand.)

ELZIE. I'm sorry. Didn't know you was here.

    (He stares.)

TONI. *(Not rushing to cover herself.)* Don't matter. But you can turn around please.

ELZIE. *(He doesn't.)* Didn't know you had something so nice up under all those clothes you be wearing.

TONI. *(Covering herself with her arms.)* Why you do that Elzie?

ELZIE. You pretty.

TONI. Thank you. Don't you get tired always trying to say wha'chu think people expect you to? You can turn round now please.

ELZIE. *(Turning around.)* Ain'chu tired workin' so hard not to care.

TONI. Don't know wha'chu mean.

ELZIE. Why you ain't try to fit in a little? Just strange as you wanna be and like you're proud of it.

TONI. Go to hell, Elzie.

ELZIE. You go to hell.

TONI. No one like a lie Elzie.

ELZIE. My business ain't nobody's business. An' I don't know whatchu talkin' 'bout anyway.

TONI. I mean you like boys, and I don't think it would matter so much if you wasn't trying to put up a front all the time.

ELZIE. You so simple. Only reason you don't get your ass kicked all the time walkin' round here, wearing suits, actin' like you a man, is 'cause you got all us around you to protect you all the time. You have no idea who I am, an' what I have to be careful 'bout. I would advise you to mind your business and don't be thinkin' you and me is the same.

TONI. I know we ain't the same.

ELZIE. How 'bout you don't speak to me again, an' I'll keep my mouth closed 'bout what we both know's the truth about you.

TONI. I don't know what you mean.

ELZIE. I been keeping your secret all this time and you gone turn on me like this.

TONI. I wasn't turning on you, I was just trying to say it's okay.

ELZIE. Well, you gone let my shit loose, got no reason to hold onto yours.

TONI. Honestly, I don't know what you talking about.

ELZIE. You think I'm stupid? I'm a pitcher, Toni. These stupid mothfuckas might not can see it, but I see how those pitches be comin' to you easy, always somewhere between the fourth and sixth innings. Going on two years now. So you stay quiet and stay the hell away from me.

> (**TONI** *moves to Jack's.*)

TONI. Aury, I don't understand what's wrong with everybody.

ALBERGA. Baby, let's go down to the courthouse, make you an honest woman, and you can be done with it.

TONI. Why would you think I'd wanna be done?

ALBERGA. You just said...

TONI. Millie, you hear what he sayin' to me?

> (**MILLIE** *puts her stockings on in her area, back to* **TONI**, *not responding. Her light fades.*)

Ernie Scott...earned twenty-five RBIs in as little time as most players were able to –

ALBERGA. I said STOP THAT.

TONI. Well you stop. Because I'm not ready. Millie –

> (**MILLIE** *enters, picks up the robe, and exits without speaking.*)

Millie don't talk to me these days. Seem I always make someone mad and then don't even know what I did. But she ain't tryin' to tell me.

*(It's morning on the bus. **STRETCH** walks on.)*

STRETCH. Wake up y'all. You all know what today is.

JIMMY. Payday!

ELZIE. Take your voice down.

SPEC. Could you at least give the sun a chance to rise?

> **(STRETCH** *walks down the aisle, gives each* **MAN** *a small stack of bills, then waits for each to peel off three dollars.)*

TONI. Each payday, Stretch takes a portion of the boys' pay to send to their families.

> *(When* **STRETCH** *gets to* **JIMMY**, **JIMMY** *acts like he doesn't see him. It's a standoff, the bus gets quiet. Finally:)*

JIMMY. *(Mumbling.)* I need you to pass over me today.

STRETCH. Speak up boy. I can't hear you.

JIMMY. Need you to pass over me. I'll be good for it next week.

STRETCH. But how your woman gonna put food in the mouths of those babies this week?

TONI. Stretch, I can put in for him...

(To **JIMMY**.*)* You can get me next week...

WOODY. He's just feeling tight 'cause he got the bad end of a poker game.

JIMMY. They set me up.

SPEC. They set you up?

WOODY. How you gonna call that a set-up Jimmy?

JIMMY. Could just feel something wasn't right.

WOODY. First all, it's stupid 'cause you ask can you play in a game you wasn't invited into...

JIMMY. Then why you didn't say something?

SPEC. We tried to save your ass.

WOODY. I said, "Come on Jimmy, we don't have time, bus 'bout to leave" –

JIMMY. But we wasn't leavin' for another hour or so.

ELZIE. Damn it's a good thing you got a good arm Jimmy.

>(**JIMMY** *looks like he's about to cry and the* **PLAYERS** *let him be.*)

>(**JIMMY** *moves over and sits next to* **TONI**.)

JIMMY. *(Whispering.)* You mind you work with me tomorrow on my swing again?

TONI. Ssshhh. Don't let them hear you asking me that. And you just got out the hot seat. Get some sense.

WOODY. You Toni's best friend now, Jimmy?

TONI. No... I just called him over here to ask him 'bout his mama.
(To audience.) I don't know Jimmy's mama. We about to *play the dozens*.

>(*Beat.*)

It's alright. It's just a game.

STRETCH. How is Jimmy's mama Toni?

TONI. You tell me Stretch.

STRETCH. Jimmy mama so fat –

ALL (EXCEPT WOODY). *(To* **STRETCH**.*)* How fat is Jimmy mama?

STRETCH. Jimmy mama sooo fat she stepped on a one-dollar bill and it turned into four quarters.

JIMMY. *(Whispering to* **TONI**.*)* Why you sell me out like that?

>(**TONI** *hits him on the leg.*)

TONI. Woody, how fat's Jimmy mama?

WOODY. Don't give a fuck how fat Jimmy's mama is.

>(*Beat.*)

STRETCH. ...

KING. Jimmy mama so old and so fat, that when God said, "Let there be light," had to tell her, "Move out the way."

WOODY. Okay okay okay. Jimmy mama so fat...

JIMMY. I thought you didn't care about my mama?

WOODY. Don't give a shit 'bout your mama but your mama soo fat gotta take two trains and a bus to get to her good side.

SPEC. It's alright Jimmy, 'cause yo mama got a nice personality...

ELZIE. 'Cept she so fat she ate it!

JIMMY. Yeah. Okay okay. Well, your daddy so bow-legged and your mama so knock-kneed when they walk down the street it spell the word "OX."

> *(The PLAYERS file off the bus, circle around it, and file back on.)*

TONI. And so it go, 'til someone else do something stupid and it's their fat mama, or stupid daddy, or dumbass brother. Day three of playing in hard rain that seemed like it should cool things off, but was just warm and comin' in sideways. It's a ridiculous way to play ball, but the owners aren't about to call it, and we want the paychecks too, so you play your nine innings and almost don't care who win, so long as you can get somewhere and get dry. Anyhow, we playin' this town not so far way from Madam Mamie's and I already decided I'm gon' sleep in my wet clothes on the bus, 'cause I ain't got the heart to face Millie's silence.

> *(TONI comes out of the dugout, surprised to see MILLIE there.)*

You came? I ain't never seen you at a game. And you come out on a night like this?

(To audience.) Millie don't say it, but I know she don't like the looks the wives give her, pulling their kids back behind their skirts...

MILLIE. I guess I wanted to see what all the fuss was about.

> *(Beat.)*

TONI. Your dress is pretty. You look very nice.

MILLIE. Thank you. Now that I seen you play I understand. I had a man like that once. I was real good at him. And he was real hard on me and it felt good anyway somehow. 'Til one day it didn't. I still think about him. He was maybe the best thing I was ever good at. And he was not easy.

TONI. I'm sorry for what I said.

MILLIE. What did you say?

TONI. Don't know...but I am going to work real hard not to say those kinds of things again.

MILLIE. Alright then.

(*Beat.*)

TONI. I did it Millie.

MILLIE. You married him and didn't invite me?

TONI. No. I mean *I did it*, we did it.

MILLIE. Hallelujah Hosanna. And...?

TONI. Batting average done gone up thirty points.

(*She joins* **ALBERGA** *at Jack's. He hands her a drink.*)

ALBERGA. Toni, I gave you a nice ring. I've shown you a new kind of fun that it seems you're enjoying. Is there any reason, under the sun, you can think of for why we shouldn't be married.

TONI. (*To audience.*) I really couldn't think of a reason. So, we got married... I'm hoping you don't mind I don't take you through the wedding.

(*A* **PLAYER** *brings* **TONI** *a veil that she puts on over her baseball hat.*)

There was lace. Lots of it. White. We said our words, (*They pose for a picture, flash of the camera.*) did the rings, (*Another pose, another flash.*) and that happened. (*Pose. Flash.*)

(*Beat, taking off veil.*) Well, if this being somebody's wife thing wasn't enough to adjust to, Syd decides to play me for one inning less. Talking 'bout how it look bad, people always speculating 'bout if I'm in a family way and he playin' me too hard. Before I got married I was just Toni. Now I'm a girl.

(*Mumbling as she crosses to* **MILLIE.**) As though I cain't be in the game more'n five innings 'cause I'm gonna trip over my pussy bottom of the sixth or something.

MILLIE. Things can stretch out if you use them too much.

TONI. Stop it Millie.

MILLIE. I know we've talked about it to death. I know Toni. It just don't seem like you're having fun. Syd treats you like dirt, the boys still wish you wasn't there, and you running round taking care of Alberga on top of it all.

TONI. Alberga's easy. He a grown man, he know how to dress and feed himself.

MILLIE. But ain't chu just a little tired sweetie?

TONI. I cain't be tired Millie.

MILLIE. Sho you can...

TONI. Tell me how I'm gonna be tired? What I look like if I just hang up my cleats and go be barefoot in his kitchen. An' what if I like it in there. Then who am I Millie?

MILLIE. You always tellin' me what I do ain't who I am.

TONI. I just said that to make you feel better.

MILLIE. You a fool.

TONI. Serious though, what if baking pancakes makes me happy?

MILLIE. That would be tragic, it got out somethin' other than baseball makes Toni happy.

> (**TONI** *takes her stance at bat.*)

TONI. *(To* **MILLIE**.*)* I think Alberga's making me soft. An' the boys can smell it on me.

MILLIE. Toni.

TONI. Yeah?

MILLIE. You don't bake a pancake.

> (**TONI** *talks to* **MILLIE** *as she strikes out. The* **PLAYERS** *on the bench are not pleased...*)

TONI. I know that Millie.

> (*She swings and misses, her frustration mounting.*)

UMPIRE. *(Offstage.)* STRIKE ONE!

MILLIE. You said bake.

TONI. You know what I was sayin'.

(*She swings and misses.*)

UMPIRE. (*Offstage.*) STRIKE TWO!

MILLIE. You know what *I* was sayin'.

(**TONI** *swings, misses.*)

UMPIRE. (*Offstage.*) YOU'RE OUT!

TONI. DAMMIT!! DAMMIT!! DAMMIT ALL TO HELL!!

(*She throws her bat, kicks the dirt, and walks into the dugout.* **MILLIE**'s *light fades.*)

WOODY. Why you can't hit a baseball, Toni?

KING. Why you wanna be an asshole, Woody?

WOODY. She's playing like a girl.

TONI. Just trying to even my stats out so they don't be making you look so bad.

WOODY. You wouldn't have to do all that kick'n in the dirt and yelling at the umpire if you'd just hit the ball from time to time.

STRETCH. Stop it Woody.

WOODY. What, it's okay for her to say whatever bull she wants to me, but I speak the truth and you all want me to be quiet.

KING. I don't care what you say Woody, it's just the sound of your voice what makes me want to hurt you.

WOODY. You can all go to hell.

ELZIE. So why cain't you hit a ball today Toni?

TONI. I got off my game at the top and I can't get it back Elzie.

ELZIE. Uh-huh.

(**SPEC** *stands on one of the benches, talks to the team:*)

SPEC. I'm just gone say it, to a person, you're all playin' like five-year-old girls. You're hot? You're tired? Scared you won't get laid tonight if these backwoods Negroes show you up? You all know how many people died so your rusty asses could be free and get paid to do that which you love? Do you have any sense of the sacrifices our forefathers made so that you could have what you have now. Harriet Tubman once said...

> *(He continues, low and impassioned, under* **TONI**:*)*

SPEC.	**TONI.**
"I had reasoned this out in my mind, there was one of two things I had a right to, liberty or death; If I could not have one, I would have the other; for no man should take me alive.	We in the top of the seventh, behind eight to four now, so tired we cain't see straight, and more'n a little done with it and each other. About once every season Spec does this.
To quote Ida B. Wells, one of the country's greatest orators and a selfless promoter of the race, "The miscegenation laws of the South only operate against the legitimate union of the races...	We aren't listenin' to what he's saying...but we appreciate it that all four-feet-eleven-and-a-half inches of him is here, and cares enough about anything to say it at all.

> *(Beat. When* **SPEC** *has finished:)*

TONI. So, bottom of the eighth, we rally...and surprise even ourselves when we start to take it back.

> *(Crack of a bat. Beat. Cheers.* **TONI** *jogs into the dugout, triumphant. She's hit a home run.)*

I already told you I'm not one to brag...but every now and then one has to brag. This would be one of those times. Brought in three men to win the game.

> *(She makes her way to the bus, where the* **PLAYERS** *are asleep.)*

(To audience.) Still, going on week five on the road, back-to-back games, in the hottest heatwave I can remember since, the last hottest heatwave. We're Deep South, so there's no getting off of this bus but to play and get back on it quick.

> *(Beat. Beat.)*

(Settling into her seat.) Nothing is more foul than the sweat of men what you annoyed with, and by end of the week, the smells mix and steam and stick to you, and it's just gone get worse. You like to lose your mind.

> *(She ties a scarf on her head, puts her baseball cap on top, and leans her head against her glove.* **WOODY** *moves from the back of the bus and sits down next to her.)*

WOODY. You ain't sleep Toni?

TONI. Just about. Ain't no more.

WOODY. Can we talk for a minute? Seem like we never have time to just talk.

TONI. Alright then. *(This is strange.)*

WOODY. You played good out there today.

TONI. Played hard. Don't know 'bout good. I've had better games.

WOODY. Got more hits than me.

TONI. I wasn't counting.

WOODY. 'Course you were. Like everybody else...

> *(Beat.)*

How many people you think was at the game today?

TONI. I don't know. It was a big game. Woody, it's awful late. I like this thing, whatever this is where we're talking...but could we please do that in the morning... I'm so tired.

WOODY. I'm thinkin' there was at least one thousand eight hundred fans in those bleachers. All them cheering to see you do your thing.

TONI. Yeah. They were a good crowd.

> *(Beat.)*

Woody? You got somethin' on your mind?

WOODY. I just keep doin' the math and...

TONI. See, that's where you lose me... I can't do math to save my life... My daddy used to try and tell me –

WOODY. I just keep thinking...one thousand eight hundred people, then the twenty or so from the other team, and the sixteen or so of our guys and you know what that comes to Toni?

TONI. No.

WOODY. Something in the range of one thousand eight hundred thirty-six. And that's how many folks watched you show me up today.

> *(Beat.)*

You think you're special, don't you?

TONI. That's what they always told me.

WOODY. When you in bed with your old man, how does he do it? 'Cause I'm thinkin' you'd be on top 'cause you wear the britches...or do you even do it? 'Cause some folks think you one those bulldaggers, which must make him a dandy...

So maybe you do perverted things to some girl while he watch?

> **(TONI** *hits him hard. Something between a slap and a punch. She gets enough of a piece to hurt.* **WOODY** *grabs her arm.)*

You ain't gone cry out is you Toni. Don't want them all to think you jess a girl, jess like any other girl. Tell me Toni. How you like it? 'Cause I keep having this picture in my head, fact, I'm 'bout to walk back to my seat, an' I want you to know that the picture I'll be having in my head, when I get to the back of the bus, is both of us on that pitcher's mound, all one thousand eight hundred and thirty-seven, not thirty-six, that's including your old man... So all one thousand eight hundred and thirty-seven people in that stadium watch while I bend you over.

> *(He walks to the back of the bus. **TONI** looks around to see if anyone has heard, pulls her cap down over her eyes, and tries to soothe herself. It is possible that despite her best efforts, a tear falls. By the end of the counting, she has found her footing.)*

TONI. Smokey Joe Williams, nickname: Cyclone. 1,286 innings pitched, eighty-nine wins, fifty-five losses, 3.79 ERA, 111 complete games, gave up 303 walks, struck out 769. Buck Leonard: 412 games, 1,472 at-bats, 351 runs, 471 hits, seventy-three doubles, twenty-six triples, sixty home runs, 275 RBIs, 257 base on balls, .527 slugs. Buck O'Neil: 722 times at bat, 204 hits, twenty-seven doubles, twelve triples, seven home runs, ninety-nine RBIs, average .283, .382 slugs. Willie Foster...

> *(Beat... Beat... Beat.)*

(To audience.) The best players know, and even still it's hard to do. Hard to learn. Hard to feel in your body. When a pitcher throws you a curve, it's comin' in hard and fast and feel like right between your eyes... And you know it's gonna drop, gonna drop fast, and to the left, then mosey right on through the strike zone... But when it's comin' at your face, any person, with any amount of sense, wants to pull away, lean back and swing hard. But you can't... You gotta reach into the curve. Gotta lean into it, bravely.

> *(Beat.)*

> *(In the morning, the **PLAYERS** file off the bus, lining up, backs to the audience. They are taking a piss at the side of the road. **TONI** talks to the audience from the bus. Through the course of the following, each **PLAYER** buttons up and takes a place on the bus. **TONI***

talks to **MILLIE**, *from the bus, as* **PLAYERS** *push past her, some still fastening their pants.)*

TONI. Millie, if I never had to see or smell another disgusting man, I could maybe be okay 'til the end of time. Always scratching, moving their Johnsons around, spitting. And smell like the stank of a thousand years. Even Alberga's got his own set of things that annoy me.

(**TONI** *has crossed into* **MILLIE**'s *"room."*)

MILLIE. What he do?

TONI. Lately?

MILLIE. Yeah?

TONI. He be breathin' real loud.

(She settles in. **MILLIE** *begins to press her hair.)*

Millie, I ain't been liking this...

MILLIE. Glad to hear you say it.

(Beat.)

Keep your head down.

TONI. I think Aury's dead set on making me out to be delicate. Delicate's dangerous.

(She watches as **ALBERGA** *walks toward the dugout, where the* **PLAYERS** *put away their equipment.)*

(To **MILLIE**.*)* First off, I don't like it that Alberga be showin' up unannounced at the dugout sometime. I don't be going into his office, actin' like they my friends.

MILLIE. What they be talkin' about?

TONI. I don't know... I have to walk clear over to the ladies' bathrooms on the other side of the stadium just to get changed... But the other day, when I get back...seems like things is off. That maybe Woody and Aury had words. Later I asked Alberga –

MILLIE. You shouldn't have done that.

TONI. People need to stop telling me what to do.

(In the dugout.)

ALBERGA. How've you been Woody?

WOODY. Alright I guess. You?

ALBERGA. Same old, same old. You all looked good out there today. Haven't been able to get to games as much lately, things been so busy with work.

>   *(Beat.)*

Guess you wonderin' why I came over.

>   (**WOODY** *doesn't answer.*)

I need you to help me with something. Alright?

>   *(Beat.)*

I said, alright?

WOODY. Yes, sir.

ALBERGA. I'm tryin' to figure out if your problem is you cain't get in her britches or that she's more of a man in her britches than you ever been in yours. You don't need to answer. Just know this, I been in those britches, and let me tell you... Ain't no man but me 'tween those strong legs... It's sweet, an' it's mine. You mess with my wife again an' I swear I'll kill you...not 'cause she can't... but because it'd be my pleasure.

TONI. *(Storming into their house.)* You had no right to say all that to Woody.

ALBERGA. What?

TONI. I know what you did and it wasn't yours to get into.

ALBERGA. It's time to walk away –

TONI. I don't do that! If I was someone who walks I wouldn't be here baking you pancakes.

ALBERGA. You don't mean that.

>   *(Beat.)*

TONI. Try me.

ALBERGA. I hate what you doin' to your body. Those are the only knees you get for the rest of your life.

TONI. My knees don't belong to you. Never give a shit about my knees when I get on them in front of you.

ALBERGA. I'm just trying to take care of you.

TONI. THEY ARE MY KNEES!!

ALBERGA. You have lost your mind.

TONI. Before you put this ring on my finger you was liking the me that plays ball.

ALBERGA. But you wasn't my wife. I'm telling you, it's time to leave.

TONI. Telling me? Who do you think you are?

ALBERGA. YOUR HUSBAND! I will not have my wife coming home bruised and bleeding and smelling like the sweat of other men.

TONI. Just like Woody. You was fine with me playing until they started calling you Mr. Stone.

ALBERGA. If you don't do it, I'll do it for you.

TONI. Over my dead body –

ALBERGA. I'm not asking you. It's done.

TONI. I'd like to see you try.

(To audience.) And would you know, nigger calls Syd, tells him he's taking me out. And Syd doesn't bat an eye. Just says okay. Like it's Aury's decision, and I got 'til end of day to pack up my stuff.

> *(She looks to the **PLAYERS** for help. It's just like the boys with Coach Gabby. The **PLAYERS** avert their eyes, gather their equipment, and exit. **SPEC** remains.)*

> *(**TONI** packs up her things, angrily. Making as much noise as she can. Needing **SPEC** to say something.)*

> *(A moment. Finally:)*

You ain't got nothin' to say Spec?

SPEC. Whatchu want me to say Toni?

TONI. You see what they did to me. I thought at least you would understand.

SPEC. Why?

TONI. Just, 'cause –

SPEC. "Success is to be measured not so much by the position...one has reached in life –

TONI & SPEC. "– As by the obstacles which he has overcome."

TONI. Booker T. You read it yesterday.

SPEC. "Man's greatness consists in his ability to do and the proper application of..."

TONI. Well, I'm not a man.

SPEC. "I would fight for my liberty...

TONI. Stop!

SPEC. "– And if the time came for me to go...

TONI. Spec!

SPEC. "– The Lord would let them take me." – Harriet Tubman.

TONI. So I'm just s'posed to let them put me out to pasture, 'cause Harriet Tubman said so? Harriet Tubman don't know me.

    (Beat.)

'Cause she dead.

SPEC. Toni.

TONI. I'm just s'posed to let them take it away. I thought you knew me better than that.

    *(**SPEC** gathers his book, getting up to go.)*

SPEC. I thought I did.

TONI. So you mad too?

    (Beat.)

WELL I'M SORRY THEN! Folks wanna all the time be mad at me. An' I'm doin' all kinds of jumpin' jacks, tryin' to understand why and what I did, and figure out what they saying, so I don't do it again...when someone work that hard to hear what I'm saying?

SPEC. You did it Toni. Damn, go gracefully. Some of us don't get to.

TONI. I'm tired.

SPEC. Who ain't tired Toni?

(*He exits.*)

TONI. Spec!

(*He's gone.*)

Millie?

MILLIE. Already told you what I think.

TONI. What if I can't –

MILLIE. Could come work with me... Make your mama real proud.

(*Beat.*)

What happened to, "You can do anything if you work hard enough."

(*Beat.*)

Was you meaning that only for baseball?

(*Beat.*)

Girl. Get outta here, I got a...client, 'bout to come. You'll be okay, Toni. Just gotta decide to.

TONI. (*To audience.*) Millie was right. Spec was right. Alberga wasn't all the way wrong either – to be tired of sharing me with this thing that has always had my heart more than there's room for anyone. Tried real hard to put myself in somebody else's shoes.

(*Beat.*)

It didn't work. I don't wear other people's shoes. That's nasty. So instead I decided, hell, if I could put on a skirt and skate for a year, I'd might as well put the apron on for someone I love.

(*Beat.*)

Turns out I'm okay in the kitchen. Recipes are like rules, you do what it says, it come out pretty much the way it's supposed to. I built Aury a new front porch, wall-to-wall bookshelves on each side of the fireplace, hell, I built the fireplace.

(Beat.)

But I felt like the weight of a thing, was missing.

*(**ALBERGA** moves into the room.)*

ALBERGA. Fireplace looks nice Toni. What you've done here, real nice.

TONI. I found that mantelpiece in a salvage yard. You like I painted it gray, huh?

(Long pause.)

What about those?

(Long pause.)

They call those corbels.

(Pause.)

You like those?

(Pause.)

They nice gray too.

ALBERGA. You always choose well.

TONI. Sky was clear, but it smelled like it was 'bout to rain, day Satchel pitched me that curve. He said:

ALBERGA & TONI. "How do you like it..."

TONI. And I said, "It doesn't matter" –

ALBERGA. Yes. And you hit a single. Best day of your life.

(Beat.)

Is there something you need to say to me Toni?

(Beat.)

TONI. I take care of you good, don't I Aury?

ALBERGA. 'Course you do.

TONI. And I do it not resentful or nothin', right?

ALBERGA. You were pretty evil for a while there.

TONI. Well that was foul, how you went up behind me to Syd...but since then, I came around.

ALBERGA. Indeed.

TONI. I liked the work I spent on you this last year. But now you gotta let me go back.

ALBERGA. When did you start waiting for anyone to "let" you do anything?

TONI. Since I got married and swore before my family and God, that I'd obey you and all that.

> *(Beat.)*

Part of me is dying, Aury.

> *(Beat.)*

It seemed like you was proud of me 'til you gave me a ring.

Did you really think this little piece of gold would make me someone else? Plenty of girls what don't wear pants and aren't only happy when they got dirt under their nails. So why you ain't just picked one of them?

ALBERGA. They wasn't you.

TONI. Aury, I'm gonna make like I'm the ball and you're the bat now.

> *(She kisses him, a long, slow kiss.)*

> *(**ALBERGA** exits and the **PLAYERS** walk on in a line, crossing the stage past **TONI** as they make their way to a field that's somewhere off stage right.)*

TONI. Boys, I'm back.

JIMMY. Toni!

SPEC. Was you gone Toni?

WOODY. Thought you just went to the bathroom to take care some womanly things.

STRETCH. You look good, Toni. Marriage suits you.

ELZIE. Put a little weight on, in all the right places. Very nice.

KING. Toni, how fat is Jimmy's mama?

JIMMY. Hey!

WOODY. *(Offstage.)* We still talkin' 'bout Jimmy's mama mothafuckas?

TONI. *(To audience.)* Here it is. I did something that no one else before me had been able to do. I did it smart and I did it pretty and I didn't listen when they said I can't do a thing. I did a thing. And then I did this other thing, that I didn't know was in me. And then I remembered, when they said I couldn't do a thing, and I did that... And they said I couldn't do a thing, and I did that too... and then they said I couldn't do a thing. And *you* know what I did. I reached. Turns out between the weight of a thing, and the reach... There's breath...and in that breath is life.

    *(**TONI** exits.)*

End of Play